PRIVATE WAR

by

GORDON CLARK

Target Practice

Light flooded out of the roller door of the rundown warehouse illuminating the two cars parked there, their boots wide open and waiting expectantly for the arrival of the cargo from within. The scene was bare of people, but even from their hiding place just forty yards away, they could hear music from a radio blaring out some nondescript rap artist. All of the surrounding buildings were dark, hardly a surprise at gone midnight.

"Trojan Two, what can you see?" the lead of the police firearms unit whispered into his radio. He knew there was no real need to speak so softly, but habits were hard to break. He looked over his shoulder at the five other officers in his team, knowing that they were ready to go, hyped up.

"We haven't seen anyone since the cars arrived," Trojan Two reported from their rooftop location two buildings away. "They parked up, opened the cars ready to load, then disappeared into the building."

Trojan One looked back to the vehicles, wondering what was taking their targets so long. Had there been some sort of a problem? Had they just decided to take a break, a cup of tea and a pizza with their colleagues? "Trojan Three. Do you have anything happening back there?" he asked, knowing that a decision needed to be made and soon. Someone would see them if they waited around long enough, the advantage of surprise gone.

Intel had led them here, one of their undercover policemen getting the nod that the Albanian gang were ready to release a hundred kilos of cocaine onto London's streets, the street value around about forty pounds per gram. The margins were massive: buying the stuff at just four thousand pounds a kilo, selling it on at forty thousand pounds. Yes, it was a risky business, but the 'Albanian Mafia' were a tight run ship, each group made up mainly of family members. Getting information was hard, and when a chance like this came along, it had to be exploited.

The drugs had come in just east of London at Tilbury Docks, hidden under the false floor of a shipping container. Pressure had been put on the Metropolitan Police to immediately impound the steel box, arrest the driver and work backwards to the source of the drugs, somewhere in Rotterdam, but the Assistant Commissioner of Scotland Yard had bigger ambitions. He wanted the people distributing the white powder in his city. He wanted to break-up the gangs, disrupt their networks. It was a risky course of action, but if it worked out, it could mean a step-up the promotion ladder. One day, the man wanted to reach the lofty height of Commissioner.

Trojan Three were on the opposite side of the warehouse, a team of six armed officers who's task would be to stop the criminals if they fled out that way during the raid.

"We don't even have a door on this side," Three's team leader reported back. "No windows, nothing. We can see nothing, boss."

It was time to do something, and that something meant deploying his armed response unit into the warehouse. It wasn't the plan, but something had to happen. The preference would have been to jump the Albanians as they loaded their vehicles, to catch them red handed, or white handed to be more correct, the drugs being a fine snowy powder.

"All Trojan units," the lead man muttered. "We are going in. Keep us covered, but do not use your weapons unless you see a threat to life. You know the rules of engagement."

The other Trojan callsigns clicked their radio pressel switches to acknowledge the instruction. They knew the rules, even if they didn't agree with them. Waiting for the bad guys to 'threaten someone's life' meant that their engagement of the crooks would usually be too late. One of their number would already be targeted by then, possibly dead or wounded.

But rules were rules. Breaking them would possibly mean a prison sentence, even firing their weapon would mean an internal investigation as to whether it had been necessary, during which time they would be suspended from duty. It made no sense, but as everyone was well aware, law is an ass. In most of the team's minds, it was actually an arse. It increased their chances of getting hurt.

The head of the team stood, signalled to the others to spread out, keeping several metres between each of the members. Taking down six men spread over around twenty metres was much harder than shooting them all if they were in a bunch. He adjusted his body armour, felt the sweat trickle down the back of the T-shirt he wore under his dark fire retardant NOMEX suit, again checked the safety catch on his weapon, all of them now having a round in the breach of their stubby black Heckler & Koch G36C semiautomatic weapons. He released a short sigh, knowing that he couldn't put it off any longer, that it was time to move.

The team dashed across the darkened street one at a time, the others covering the officer who was on the move. They were now just thirty metres from the roller door, still not illuminated from the light pouring out of it. The leader waved a man forward into point position, took his place at number two in the advancing line, the rest following, weapon stocks into the shoulder, barrels searching forward for anything that looked out of place.

Twenty metres. Ten. Five.

The leader stopped the team, all dropping to their knees, everything they were now doing practiced a thousand times, no words needed. The lead man moved further into the light, his weapon pointed towards the door, stopping just before it, back to the wall and listening.

Just loud music from the radio, some gangster rap tune called 'Bang Bang'. Appropriate, the leader thought. If things went well, some Albanian Mafia boys were going to get a bit of 'Bang Bang'.

The point man glanced quickly back to his boss, got a slight nod, the message to move on. He swung into the doorway, his Heckler & Koch sweeping around the empty room in front of him.

Nothing. No people, no vehicle, just shelves of boxes, a forklift truck with no driver.

He let the team know his findings, the rest of them moving silently forward, joining him, also searching the place for signs of danger.

The leader indicated that they should spread out, the team grouping as they came through the bottleneck that was the roller door, all now within a five metre wide group, tactically a nightmare.

And that's when it happened.

The noise was incredible, gunshots raking over the entranceway as twenty men with MP5 submachine guns opened up as they stood from behind the packing cases and boxes, each weapon releasing up to 800 rounds a minute, the police team having absolutely no chance.

After less than thirty seconds, the shooting stopped, the acrid smell of gunshots filling the warehouse. The police team of six were all crumpled on the concrete floor, their body armour no match for such an overwhelming hail of bullets. One of the men twitched, but it was more muscle memory than life, a final attempt to remain with the living.

Outside, another thunder of shots came from up the street, then another rat-tat-tat-tat from the rear of the industrial unit.

"That should be all of them accounted for," one of the Albanians said, stating the blatantly obvious to the rest of them.

"Let's get out of here," the leader ordered. "We've made our statement, and now we should go before others arrive." He made his weapon safe, applied the safety catch. "Don't touch anything, and don't be tempted to steal anything off these bastards. Nothing should tie us to them." He walked towards the main door, watched as his other teams made their way towards the building.

Four large 4x4 Prado's made their way along the street, each vehicle able to fit seven people. The boss closed the boot of one of the two vehicles already parked there, climbed into the passenger seat, a team member taking the drivers spot.

"Mount up and get to your homes. Make sure everyone's alibi stacks up."

He closed the car door, the driver putting the car in gear and pulling away. A final glance at the dead police team and he finally allowed himself a tight smile.

"Not a bad day at the office," he said to himself.

The driver nodded, knowing that there was little else to add. The police had been getting a little too clever lately. This would knock them back a bit. A big bit.

The call had come from a rundown council estate in Barking, the caller telling the controller that there was some sort of domestic going on in the flat below them. They added that the baby was screaming blue murder, that they were concerned that the child might be getting abused or beaten, the parents both known drug users. A mobile unit was in the area, so it was a no-brainer, two uniforms driving straight to the scene.

Susan Blanchard had only been in the Met for nine months, and every call out was a new adventure for her. Pete Summerton had ten years of experience, a man not easily rattled. He'd seen most things in that time, not all of them very pleasant.

They pulled up outside of the address they'd been given, most of the apartments lit up in the early evening gloom.

"Do you want me to go up and check things out?" Sue asked, as ever dying to get on with things.

"We'll both go," Pete replied. "You can't be too careful with druggies. Seen some real shit go down with these household disturbances. Better that we're both there." He pressed the call button on the radio, let the station know that they were at the scene.

Susan opened her door, impatient to get to it. "Ready?" she asked.

Pete picked up his cap, sighed as he went for the door handle. Had he ever been that keen? Even in his early days? He couldn't remember it if he had been, and he certainly wasn't any more. All he wanted nowadays was to get to his pension pot as quickly as possible.

He didn't quite reach the handle, the whole world exploding into a mass of red and white and black, noise that killed his ears.

The Rocket Propelled Grenade blew the car to Kingdom Come, the two police officers dead before they knew anything about it. It would later come out in the follow-up interviews with locals that the Albanian Mafia controlled the whole area, selling crack cocaine and running protection rackets amongst other things. Even later, when the explosive experts pieced things together, it would show that the RPG was a part of a batch that could be traced all the way back to Albania.

The gangs were taking the fight to the police.

The fire started in a warehouse/housing conversion project close to Canary Wharf, a fire tender from the Shadwell Station sent to investigate. It wasn't much of a blaze, easily controlled by the single tender and its crew of six, the Crew Manager declining further assistance.

"Kids, I'd guess," the man reported back to Control. "Looks like some sort of accelerant to get things going, a load of wooden panels left to burn," he finished.

"We have a river police boat close by. They said they'll come and have a glance."

"I'll show them what we have," the manager replied.

It was nine at night, the lights of riverside flats reflecting off the surface of the Thames, the police launch's navigation lights giving away its progress towards the scene. The fireman turned on a large LED torch, showing his whereabouts on a small jetty, trying to save the boat crew time. The sooner he could get things done, the sooner he could get back to the station, get a few hours kip. One of his team offered him a hot mug of sweet tea, a nice touch on the cool evening. He sipped the steamy fluid, inhaling the fumes.

A sharp crack split the air off to his right, a flash in the darkness drawing his gaze. He could make out figures rushing away from the quayside around eighty metres distant, not picking out too much, his night vision ruined by both the fire and the burst of light.

A second later an explosion echoed across the water, and he turned to see the police vessel burst into flames, its navigation lights gone.

"What the fuck..." he started.

"RPG!" one of his team yelled, a recent recruit with an army service background.

The Crew Manager had no military experience himself but had seen enough news reports from Iraq and Afghanistan to know what the man meant. It still made no sense. A rocket propelled grenade here in London?

"Call Control!" the man yelled. "We need a boat out there. That thing is sinking." In front of his eyes the launch was dropping in the water, its bow suddenly tipping skywards. He felt helpless, unable to react to the incident, unable to assist anyone on the vessel. He turned his attention to where the initial flash had come from, looking for the perpetrators, but the place was now deserted.

He took out his phone, dialled 999, already knowing that it was too late.

Before him the police launch slipped backwards into the darkness of the river, the bow coming back down with a small splash, settling with only the top of the darkened cabin left in view, the shallow river hiding the rest.

"We're not fighting criminals, we're fighting an army," the Assistant Commissioner explained to the Prime Minister. "They have the men, the weaponry, and they're not restricted by the rules my people need to follow. We're fighting them with one hand tied behind our backs."

Ruth Maybank glanced at her Minister of State for Crime, Policing and Fire, hoping to receive some sort of an answer. The man merely nodded back, showing his support for the senior police officer. "I'm afraid he's right," he finally said. "The way things are right now, the police are simply becoming targets. We have to change their rules of engagement or change the way we take on the criminals."

"And changing the rules will take time and cause confusion," the policeman added. "We'll end up spending more time in court than on the beat. When is force deemed acceptable, and when is it excessive? Do we arm all of our officers, or keep the weapons with specialists? I have opinions, but I don't have answers."

"And can I ask your opinions?" Ruth replied.

The man frowned, knowing his views might not match those of his superiors. "Personally," he began, "I would arm all of our people. I've been arguing this for years. We are fighting the same people as the rest of the police forces in Europe, but we are fighting without our men even having a handgun." He paused, raised his right index finger. "This wouldn't be the opinion of the Commissioner, I hasten to add." He lowered his hand. "She wants to keep the bobby on the beat as an approachable figure, not an armed soldier."

Ruth nodded, an idea forming in her mind. "Is that perhaps the answer?" she asked, confusing the two men.

"I'm not following," the Assistant Commissioner spoke for them both.

The PM leaned back in her chair. "Do we keep the police as the friendly face, the team that offer the public assistance?" she offered. "Then support them with just what you said, the armed soldier." She leant forward to her desk, steepled her fingers. "Do we take on the bad guys with the army, not with the police? No new laws – we already use the military to support you in certain circumstances, we just extend that role." She spread her hands, inviting comment from the others.

The police officer considered the suggestion, wondering what his boss would think about it. "Let me take it up with the Commissioner," he finally relented. "But on the face of it, it could work. If we feel that something is a set-up, we send in the troops. Take on the Albanians with the army."

The Minister for the police also nodded. "Fight fire with fire," he said.

Ruth glanced at her watch. She needed to move, her schedule totally chaotic. "Let's leave it at that then," she said. "Talk to your people, give me a summary of pros and cons for the idea. Let's meet again in a day or so." She stood, ready to go. "Fix something with my PA," she added, heading for the door. It was time to get to Westminster, another battering on the cards from the opposition expected at PMs Question Time. They always had something new to complain about.

Sometimes she wondered why she'd ever decided to get back into politics. In the beginning, it used to be fun, but now it was just hard work. Whatever you did, it was always wrong according to somebody.

Another day, another dollar, she told herself as she headed out to the waiting car. And just another year…

Janet Anderson wasn't just the head of MI6, she was also the PMs closest friend, their relationship established all those years ago when they'd studied together at the London School of Economics. Whenever Ruth had an idea that needed researching, Janet was her first port of call, even if the subject was nothing to do with her job.

"Do you think it could work?" the PM asked after outlining the discussion that she'd just left. "We need to do something about the Albanian gangs, and the police aren't structured for what is rapidly becoming a war on their people."

Janet was well aware of the problem the boys in blue were facing, had her own people trying to cut off the supply routes that the gangs were using, not just for drugs, but also for people trafficking and the sex trade. One of the poorest countries in Europe certainly had a lot to answer for.

"It could work," she answered evasively. "But would the military want to get involved? They're already stretched to breaking point, what with NATO commitments and helping out as ambulance drivers, bin men, and whatever else they get roped into. It's like whenever there's a problem, just wheel in the army. I'm not sure that some of your senior military figures would go with it," she added.

Ruth nodded to herself, her own sentiments quite similar. The poor squaddie had to be a 'jack of all trades', with most of them not what they'd joined up for, that was for sure. "So you think it's a no?" she asked.

Janet frowned. Her friend sounded beaten, something that she'd sensed too often in recent months. The job was getting to her, and Janet wondered if she'd even stick it out until the next election. "Let me have a chat with your favourite soldier," she said, keeping the door open and fanning the flame of hope. "If anyone might have an idea of how to target those bastards, then Alex has to be your man."

It was a shot in the dark, but it reduced the pressure on Ruth Maybank. At least for a short time.

Practice Makes Perfect

Alex stormed into the Killing Rooms, eyes searching swiftly and efficiently for targets, double tapping his shots at each of the human sized shapes that presented themselves in doorways, next to windows, appearing from behind chairs. Interspersed with the Figure Eleven style targets were SAS troopers, most of them grinning as their boss tried desperately to knock out the bad guys while avoiding a friendly fire incident. It was a strange reaction when you considered that all of the shooting was done with live ammunition, but the elite troops had all taken part in it, conditioning them for when it was actual enemy fire coming their way. Being in close proximity to death helped you learn to live with it.

"Okay, exercise over!" the staff sergeant running the training yelled as Alex blew away the last of the enemy. "Make your weapon safe."

Alex pulled back the slide, making certain that no bullets were in the breach, removed his magazine and presented the directing staff with a view into the pistol. "Clear!" the NCO shouted to make himself heard. Alex released the slide, pulled out his ear defenders. He grabbed a seat, drained now that the adrenalin was lessening. Live firing always raised the heart rate, even after all these years.

"You should give this up, boss," one of the troopers said with a grin. "You're getting too old for this sort of thing. Stick to driving your desk. Leave this gung-ho stuff to us lads."

Alex showed the man his middle finger, also smiling. A part of him was in agreement with the youngster, but as an ex-NCO himself, the Colonel of 22nd SAS Regiment didn't believe in making others do what he couldn't handle himself. "Maybe I'll slot you next time round," he threw back. "Save the cookhouse a few mega-sized meals."

"At least the boss hit all of the targets," the staff sergeant added, joining the rapport. "Unlike some that I know."

"Can you guys get my Glock back to the armoury for me please?" Alex asked. "It's time for this old boy to get back to steering the desk again. Let me make sure that you all get paid at the end of the month."

"I'll sort it boss," the trooper said, taking the gun.

"Thanks lads." Alex wiped a sheen of sweat from his brow, collected his jacket from by the door. Checking his phone, he spotted that he'd missed a call from Janet Anderson. Though old friends, he knew that a call from the head of MI6 probably meant something bad.

"No rest for the wicked," he told himself, leaving the training area.

He considered calling there and then, decided it would at least wait until he'd reached his office. He desperately needed a shot of caffeine before talking about anything too serious.

"Use the military to take on the Albanians?" he asked, confirming he was hearing things right. "I thought that would be a police firearms team task."

Janet spoke on her secure line, not wanting the idea they discussed to be picked up by any eavesdroppers. "It's an idea, Alex, just a possibility. What's your views on it? Could it work?"

The soldier paused, thinking about what he knew of the problem. He had to be honest; the groups recent operations had been more like those of terrorists than gangsters, deliberately targeting the police force. Their actions had been no less than murderous. "They've been fairly barbaric recently," he said, deciding that it was the best word to describe things without bringing in personal feelings. "If they were terrorists, then you would call on us to deal with them, so in a way it wouldn't be so wrong to utilise special forces." He pursed his lips, wondering whether to say more. He would actually love a crack at them, to face them on even terms. "It's just that we couldn't offer cover to every police call out. It would tie up too many men, something that I just don't have."

"You mean we would need selective targeting," the head of MI6 allowed. "Perhaps we use MI5 to gather intel, maybe my people for European operations, then use the SAS to flush them out." It was more work for all parties, but it was something that they all dealt with anyway, at least to some degree. "We find the threats, you sort them out."

Alex nodded to himself. It wasn't quite their normal modus operandi, but it wasn't too far from it. Well-armed criminals operating within the UK weren't so different from radicalised terrorists. They killed people. "It's an option," he conceded.

"Let me have a chat with Ruth," Janet replied. "Nothing set in stone, but something that she might like to sound out with others." It would also give her a chance to talk to MI5 to see what they had on the subject. They might even have some undercover operatives operating within the Albanian groups. Everything would help.

"I'll wait for your call," Alex agreed. It was time he also did some research. Military intelligence also had their sources.

In the meantime, he had a unit to run.

He fired up his laptop, signed into his account. An opening dashboard offered him an overview of the latest reports from his troops on the ground, dotted around the globe in places of tension and trouble. It also gave him an overview of available forces, both from the Special Air Service and the Special Boat Service, and also from the Reserve regiments.

Soldiers were out there, but it didn't make great reading. The world never seemed to be at rest, was always in conflict with itself somewhere.

"Let's try and find out what we can possibly do for Ruth," he muttered to himself.

Fighting Back

Luan Shehu was the head of the 'family', the main man in the London region. His public business interests were highly varied – a string of self-service laundrettes, a couple of pubs, take away food outlets, lap dance bars, and run down hotels. Each provided a source of money that was not easily traced, that could drastically vary on a daily basis. Each business allowed money to 'disappear' from the system, to hide its true source. In a nutshell, each was a perfect front to launder his 'less public' interests.

He was a big bully of a man, his gym days and muscle building steroids all in the past, his body now running to fat and looking like that of a nightclub bouncer. The skin on the back of his bald head looked a little like that on a bulldogs face.

Shehu had a finger in many pies, some within the UK, others across mainland Europe, largely in Albania itself, Italy and Holland. Girls from the old eastern bloc were largely routed through the homeland, often flown into Britain in plain view of the authorities, generally believing that they were escaping their own homes to live a better life. The promised jobs never came, their handlers removed their freedom by taking their travel documents, and within no time at all, they were working for the lap dance bars. Escort agencies and prostitution were only a short step from there. Within days of arriving in the UK, many wished to be back in the hovel that had been their home. A hovel that didn't rape them.

And it wasn't only women. Luan also supplied men, boys, young girls. Money was money. Some sick bastard would always pay.

The man controlled central London, his extended family tight, difficult for the authorities to infiltrate. All senior associates were directly related to him, even the less important gang members at least from the homeland. Local recruitment was only done on an ad-hoc basis, people to be used for a specific job and then dumped. Family meant loyalty, in London and back home, and punishment for breaking that trust was often death, or at least a serious beating. It produced a code of honour, an understanding amongst the people involved. It was an unwritten contract that controlled your life. You couldn't escape it. You were in, or you were out. And once you were in, there was no way out.

His campaign against the Met Police was bearing fruit, his daily operations receiving less interference than before. The kids of today were weak, this 'woke' generation not willing to put their lives on the line like the generations of the past. 'Bulldog' spirit was now served in a bottle and called gin.

He grinned at the thought, considered using it in his next briefing with senior staff. "We have besa, they have gin," he could hear himself saying. Besa was the word that the Albanians used to describe trust. It was a strong word.

Pulling himself back to the task at hand he checked a message on his mobile phone, the code meaning nothing to anyone, even if it should be intercepted by the snoops down in Cheltenham.

Another load of the purest cocaine was on its way at this very minute to Southampton Docks, just another of the UK's leaking entry points. You simply can't check every container, not in the tens of thousands that enter the country every week. And even if you could, you'd need to fully unpack each one, find the hiding places secreted within them. Border Force were batting on a losing wicket, that was certain. And when needed, a small backhander was always another possibility.

It was time to get his lieutenants together for a meeting – known colloquially as a Bajrak - to agree the requirements of their individual districts. They would then organise their Kryetar – or underbosses – who would pass down orders to their distributors, who in turn would arrange supply to the pushers selling on the street corners, in the nightclubs, brothels, and pubs. He would then get them to pull in the funds, plan for the next delivery.

This was where he made his money, not in the abuse of girls and boys, protection rackets, nor the legitimate businesses that all fell under his command. Drugs were the key. A multi-million pound empire that never seemed to contract, just endlessly expand.

He typed his own coded message into the cell phone, selected the group that needed to receive it, and pressed send.

Shehu's mafia Krye gathered together in an abandoned factory unit on the eastern outskirts of the city, over a mile away from the closest inhabited housing. Holding a meeting like this of his senior people could never be done using Zoom Meetings, or Microsoft Teams: that was the best way to get caught out by the eavesdropping authorities, to get locked in a prison cell for eternity. Forcing the gang to make their way here from as far away as Heathrow was just another way to reinforce discipline, to remind them exactly who was in charge.

"Within the next two days we will get another batch of coke coming in from Southampton," he explained to the assembled group, all of them wrapped up in dark padded jackets to hold off the night's chill, his words coming out in clouds of silver condensation. He glanced around the men, not a single female in the elite company. None of them dared to look away, but all made the point of showing interest without appearing to present a threat. A threat would be eliminated.

"I'll need to know your requirements, so get amongst your people, get an idea for trends, new markets, opportunities. I'm expecting a hundred and fifty kilos," he added. A series of silent nods greeted the announcement. There was nothing new in the request, but they all knew that they were expected to search for new income streams, new work. It was no different from any other business.

"The stuff we're getting is clean, ultra-pure. Make certain that your Kryetar understand that it should stay that way. Blend it, by all means, but make certain that nothing bad goes in. A bad batch will lose us business." Shehu understood that blending was a part of the process, making 'more' of the drug by adding other ingredients, such as baking soda and talc. He also knew that some dealers added much worse, that occasionally things went wrong. Having your customers dying on you wasn't great for business, but it also had the added disadvantage of drawing the attention of the authorities into the affected region.

"Will we also be launching any false flag operations?" one of the Krye asked. "I can offer some manpower if needed."

Shehu gave a short nod. This was a man that he trusted, a son of a cousin twice removed, but family all the same. "Not on the same scale as the last one," he replied. "I will get in touch with a few of you though, ask you to put out some rumours of where the delivery won't take place." He spat onto the concrete floor. "We know that someone is slipping information to the scum. We can use this operation to see where that info is getting out."

"And then we irradicate it," the same man replied, almost a question.

"And then we irradicate it," Shehu agreed.

Shehu had a good idea where his problem was coming from, had been watching certain people for some time now. If he was right, the problem wasn't family, it was where they'd employed outsiders to do some of the dirty work. That was a bad thing, but it was also a good one – you never want to be in a position where you can't trust your own flesh and blood. If the problem was outsiders, then he could still trust the clan.

They utilised Nigerian muscle at some of the clubs and brothels, big men that generally stopped punters from even considering causing trouble, never mind starting it. They were big beasts, but their loyalty went about as far as their next payday. They'd sell their grannies to get an extra couple of quid. And selling insider info to the police would be a no brainer for them. Money for nothing.

"Let a few people know that the drugs will be coming through your club," he told one of his people. "Keep it to a fairly tight circle, just the head barman, the chief bouncer. Watch them closely and report back."

He made the same call to another three of his establishments, all ones that utilised outside labour.

If his hunch was right, he would see action in the next day or so.

Ogadinma Abara stood back as the firearms team barged past him, their weapons sweeping arcs around the entranceway to the club. He had considered not coming to work that night, to lying up, perhaps even finding another job, but he knew that failing to show-up would have simply thrown suspicion his way. It was better to be there, to blag it. He pressed the alarm button by the door, letting the management know that they had a problem. Another attempt to deflect the blame.

The police were past him now, possibly tipped off that he was the source, not treating him as a threat. That wasn't good – he grabbed the man at their rear by the vest that held his Kevlar body armour, pulled him back and got the butt of a Heckler & Koch in his guts for the trouble.

'That will be on CCTV,' he told himself, doubled up and catching his breath. And that would help him in the long run he reasoned.

The police crew continued on into the club, a second team sledging down the back door, approaching from the far side. Behind the weapons team, a bunch of uniform followed, and behind them a search team. If the rumour was correct, somewhere in this complex of pole dancers, prostitutes, and punters, was a hundred and fifty kilo stash of cocaine, street value in the order of six million British pounds. It might cost them a snitch, but for that sort of result it was worth it. There were plenty of others out there that would grass-out their grandmothers for a small payout. They'd get another one.

Dren Sula had hoped against this happening, but at the same time was well aware that Shehu's instincts were rarely wrong. His head doorman had been the only person he'd fed the fake intelligence to, and that meant that the big Nigerian had to be the one who'd sold them out.

"Oga," he yelled into his office phone, using Ogadinma's usual label. "What the fuck is happening out there?" Of course he knew, had watched as things developed on the various CCTV cameras around the place. He also knew that no drugs would be found anywhere on his premises, except those carried by punters. Yes, he'd get a slapped wrist for the girls plying their trade, but that was nothing. If the pigs were here, then they weren't where the real drug shipment was coming in.

"The bloody cops boss!" the Nigerian answered. "They just gave me one in the guts, the bastards."

Dren had seen that too, noticed that it had appeared to be an afterthought, something that the assault team had missed on their rush to get to the action. Once again, Dren Sula was certain that Shehu had got it right, had read the signs. "Don't panic, just stop anyone else coming in. I'll talk to them, calm things down, then we can have a proper chat once it's all done."

"Right boss."

The Albanian hoped that would stop the big Nigerian from doing a runner, keep him at his post. "Keep things cool," he added. "There'll be a bonus in it for you." That would convince the bouncer to hang around.

He hung up, pressed send on his computer. A prepared message went to Shehu, a message that Sula now deleted.

He could almost see the satisfied look on his leader's face.

Cat's got the cream.

"There's fuck all here skipper," the policeman said to his senior, his radio now switched off. "It's clean, give or take a few Toms and some punters looking for a bit of fun." He forced himself not to smile, knowing that Dan Griffin wouldn't be at all amused. "We've been set up."

Griffin knew that the man was right, knew that the small amounts of drugs they'd found were not worth taking through the courts. 'Personal use' would be the argument, and the defence team would have a field day. "Get the men together and prepare to move out," he replied. "I just want a final chat with the main man." He could at least put a frightener on the bastard, warn him that the club would be monitored for the next few months. Not that that would faze the average Albanian scumbag, he reasoned; these guys played for much higher stakes, probably earned his annual salary every bloody month.

He moved away from his team, walked into the small office where the man called Dren Sula sat at his desk checking CCTV.

"Are you done?" the Albanian asked, a crooked smile on his lips. "I have a business to run, and I have almost no customers left in it." He stood up, letting the six foot police officer see just how big he was. He'd have made a good rugby prop, a proper front rower, and his broken nose and cauliflower ears would have fitted the job too. "Did you find what you were looking for?" he added.

Dan Griffin gave a tight shake of his head, hiding his emotions as far below the surface as he could, certain that the man in front of him had plenty more to tell. It had been a set-up, a come on, something to draw police teams away from where the real action was going down. He wouldn't quite call it a false flag op, but it was definitely a distraction, a shifting of the truth. "You're free to continue with your business," he allowed, falling short of addressing the man as 'sir'. "But we'll be keeping an eye on the place, getting your licences checked out. Make sure they're in order." It was as close to a threat that he could think of without getting shafted for intimidation. Playing hard ball with one hand tied behind your back was no fun at all.

Griffin nodded to the big Albanian, turned on his heel. He needed to talk to his people, to find a better way to fight the scum. This was a battle that he'd lost. It was not the war.

Oga Abara could barely open his right eye and had no chance of opening his left, the orb that had once been an eyeball now on the room's dirty floor. He was tied to a large oak table, hands secured below the wooden top, his back resting on it. The ties were unnecessary: the Albanians had operated on both of his Achilles tendons with bolt cutters, his feet no longer his own. He couldn't walk away even if they let him go.

"Who did you talk to?" Dren Sula asked, leaning his face close to the good eye. "Names, Oga. I need names." The door to the darkened room opened, and Sula looked across to see Shehu enter. He nodded to his boss, hoping that the man would let him finish his work. "You're fucked anyway, so why not just spill it?"

The big black man tried to speak, found that his mouth was full of blood and broken teeth. He spat out the debris, taking care not to get any on his captor. That would be a bad mistake. "I told you, I don't know what you're talking about," he slurred. He knew that it wasn't an answer that was going to help him, but he was also sure that he was going to die anyway, answer or no answer.

Shehu stepped forward, staring at the slab of meat on the table before him. This was almost not a man anymore, something half dead. Sula backed off, left things to his leader.

"You may not know the names, but you must know who paid you," the mafia boss whispered, keeping himself just out of sight, staying on the Nigerian's left side. "We need to know who is trying to screw with us," the man continued, his voice rough from years of smoking, his accent hard.

Abara turned his head, trying to see his new torturer. Something told him that this man was the leader, the man in charge. Perhaps he could strike a deal, save his life? Perhaps...

He jerked as cold water splashed on to his face and chest, his shirt already torn open. "It's a punter who comes here every so often," he rushed out, hoping to avoid whatever the new pain might be. He wondered if the fluid was maybe acid, that it was even now starting to burn away his skin.

"Name," the man ordered.

"I don't have a name, but he pays me a hundred quid to let him know if I hear of anything that might be serious!" He knew that he had to try and help, that his life depended on it.

"I need a way to identify him," the man said softly, as though conducting an interview with a new barmaid.

Abara wished that he had a name, even better an address, something to give the men that seemed determined to take his life. "CCTV!" he yelled out. "Look at the CCTV. Two nights ago. A man with a bald head. A goatee beard with beads in it." He spat out more blood, not caring where it went anymore. Something was happening, and he had no idea what it was.

Two circles of metal pressed into his skin, one by his left shoulder, one just above his belt buckle. He jerked, but nothing else happened.

"Name," the voice demanded.

"I don't..." He didn't finish that sentence, body jolted off the table as an electric charge slammed through it, his wet skin burning as the electricity crossed it from one electrode to the other. His scream blocked out everything, the room, the people, the hope, and he tried to shake the steel connectors off his body.

And then it stopped, the electric current halted with a flick of a switch.

Shehu looked down on the tortured soul before him, realised that the man really had nothing more to give. With the description and the CCTV they should find their man. In all probability he would come back after a short time, see if his source was still in place. And they would be waiting for him.

He nodded to Sula, moved away from the Nigerian, the stench of blood, sweat and fear no longer giving him a buzz. He ran a finger over his throat, the entertainment over.

Dren Sula flicked the switch again after turning up the current as high as the system would allow. This time the scream lasted only a second, and then the Nigerian's heart shuddered to a stop.

"Find the man with the goatee," Shehu ordered.

Sula nodded, scores to settle.

Inspector Dan Griffin sat before his Chief Superintendent, his Chief Inspector off to one side of the meeting room table. He was still in his uniform from the raid, wishing he could get home and get showered, wash off the smell of filth that seemed to fill these brothel-cum-dance bars that he'd just left behind. He hoped that the debrief would be quick, but the seniority of the people involved indicated that it probably wouldn't. Somebody, somewhere, had a massive bee in their bonnet.

"So the tip off was just total bullshit?" the senior officer asked, something Dan had clarified once already. "Are you sure you didn't miss something?"

"Sir, we had a full team in there, took the place to pieces. We took details of everyone in the place, can be ninety-nine percent certain that it was also operating as a brothel, but there were no drugs in there."

"Less the odd packet on a punter or two for personal use," the Chief Inspector chipped in.

"Correct." The information seemed irrelevant in a meeting with the Chief Superintendent, hardly something he would want to dwell on, Dan thought.

"So we've been made to look like fools again," the man said, a statement that didn't need a response. He frowned. "And it was the Albanians again," he added, just confirming the facts.

"Yes sir."

The senior policeman thought for a second or two longer. "Inspector Griffin, I want you to take the train tomorrow up to Hereford. You will be based there for a few days, perhaps more. I'll get you contact details and an overview briefing within the next hour." He stood, pursing his lips. "I'm going to do something that I'd been avoiding, but I think that now is the time to act." He picked up a file, pushed his chair back.

"Can I ask what this is regarding, sir?" Dan asked carefully.

The Chief Superintendent nodded his head, the motion starting somewhere around the middle of his chest. A definite 'yes', Dan decided. "You're going to be seconded to the Special Air Service. You, with them, are going to take down the Albanian Mafia."

Half A Plan

Research had shown Alex something about the problems not only in London, but also around the country's other major cities, giving him a brief insight into the difficulties that the Metropolitan Police were facing when fighting a highly organised and terribly loyal bunch of criminals. Family connections were a key component to the gang's success, but their fearsome reputation added to this, and their disregard for life was enough to make even the hardest man sit up and take notice.

"Your SAS people are also hard to break because of their beliefs," a psychologist from MI5 was explaining. "They all have immense respect for one another, would do anything to protect their 'brothers,'" he said, making air punctuation marks with his index fingers. "They reach that position by all having to complete the same training, tests that would break any normal human. They go to hell and back, and all just to be a part of this 'special' team." Again the index fingers empathising his point. "And then they are in and will do just about anything to never have to leave the unit."

Janet Anderson sat listening to the briefing, her opposite number from MI5 with her. They'd heard the explanations before, knew where the shrink was going.

"These guys are similar, but not through the same process. They come from a terribly poor, terribly corrupt country, and through their own endeavours and family connections, they have risen to the top. They want to stay there, and that means they must constantly stay head of the game."

"Is there any internal fighting, something that we can use against them?" Alex asked. "We like to get inside of people's heads. Hearts and minds and all of that stuff."

"So I've read," the man confirmed. "But that's where the family thing comes in. The main characters keep brothers, cousins, in-laws, family, in all of the important roles. These form a circle around them that is totally their own." He paused. "Of course, you can't run an organisation that large with just your immediate family. They try to use fellow Albanians, bring them in to the country legally and illegally, some even on the boats across the channel. They make them take an unwritten oath. They get background knowledge on their families back home. They let them see what they are capable of." He adjusted his seat position. "It's not the same as the loyalty in your regiment, but it is probably just as strong. Fear is a massive driver."

Alex considered what the man was saying, understood it. Both sides were employing hellishly strong emotions. The Albanians were using a mix of love and hate, family and fear. His boys used respect. And if he was totally honest, also a type of love. He knew that he would gladly die to save any of his men. What greater love was there than that?

"Okay," he allowed. "So they are good, not the same as us but a deadly force all the same. Too much for the boys in blue, without making too fine a point of it and belittling the coppers." He glanced towards the two intelligence chiefs.

"And that's why we need you to get involved," Janet said with a grin.

They broke for a light lunch in the mess, the psychologist leaving for his London train shortly afterwards, only Alex and the two spy women returning to the meeting room.

"I think I have a good idea of what I'm up against, I'm just not a hundred percent sure of how I should take these people on," Alex said as they walked back from the meal. "I mean, it's not like we know when they're going to commit a crime, and we can't just go and blow away a bunch of bad blokes, simply because we 'think' they might be about to do something." He considered whether he should also have signed the inverted commas to highlight his words. It was catching.

Mary Kemp glanced his way, so far the quietest at the party, a person he hadn't met to date. "With terrorism, this is often the case, as you well know. Look across the water to Northern Ireland. We always had a good idea of who the perpetrators were, just no proof. The radicals today, the same. We have surveillance on all sorts of people, but we can't just pull them in on flaky evidence. The lawyers would rip us to shreds, cost us millions."

Janet Anderson nodded agreement. "And the same in our business," she said. "Possibly worse, as we often need to convince foreign governments to act on our suspicions, and quite often factions of that leadership will have affiliations to the terrorists. It's a tough world out there."

Alex opened the door to the offices that they were using for the day, held on to it as the women passed him. "Which all brings me back to where this conversation started – what am I meant to do?"

"Let's get into the meeting room first," replied Janet. "There should be someone there that we want you to meet."

Alex sighed. Why were things always so difficult, a web of lies and deceit, smoke and mirrors? When it came to bending the rules, he was fairly certain that there was no-one better than the head of MI6.

"Let's go," he allowed, wondering who the next wordsmith would be.

Dan Griffin waited alone in the meeting room, a cup of black coffee in his hand, pacing and looking out of the window at a pretty much empty Stirling Lines. He'd not expected to see soldiers charging around with space age weapons, abseiling from helicopters, or parachuting onto the parade ground, but he had expected to at least see the odd uniformed man doing something of a military nature. So far, he had seen people that looked just like himself, wearing civilian clothes and looking as if they belonged in one of the local boozers. They weren't particularly massive, didn't look like they could take your head off with a single bite, and didn't have commando daggers clamped in their teeth. They were just... well, normal looking.

He forced himself to sit down, knew that he'd arrived twenty minutes early. He'd had no interaction through work with the SAS but knew of their reputation. They were the best, not just one of the best. He was a big fan and being asked to present something to them had him on edge.

He heard footsteps in the corridor, watched as the door opened, was slightly shocked to see the three people who entered. He knew them all by sight, the head of MI5 through his job, the MI6 lady the same, and the SAS colonel from the odd shot of him that managed to leak to the tabloids.

Standing, he waited for them to notice him, let them take the lead.

"So Alex, this is Inspector Dan Griffin, Metropolitan Police. He works mainly with Armed Response Unit, but he has worked his way up through the ranks, seen how it all works."

The intro had come from Mary Kemp. Alex stepped forward, shook the copper's hand. "Welcome to Hereford," he offered. "Sorry if we kept you waiting."

"I was a touch early," Dan responded, also greeting Janet. He hesitated, unsure of how to proceed. "I don't have much of a brief," he added.

Kemp stepped in again, her links with the Met the strongest in the small group. "I requested that your superiors didn't muddy the waters," she said. "I think we need an out of the box solution to our problem, and having guidelines from the Commissioner wouldn't assist in that."

"Our problem being the Albanian Mafia?" Dan surmised, feeding it as a question just in case he was wrong.

Alex nodded. "That's been the topic all day, so I think you got that one right," he replied. "Though exactly what these ladies are thinking is also going to be new to me." He smiled, trying to lower the tension he was feeling from the policeman. "Perhaps one of you could fill in the gaps, especially now that the trick-cyclist has gone. That man was speaking in riddles!"

Janet realised that Alex was making the policeman more comfortable, indicated that they should all sit. "We are all very aware that the Albanians are running out of control, controlling the UK drug scene, the people trafficking, prostitution. I'm not going to pussyfoot around with introductions, we're all far too experienced for that." Janet looked to her opposite number in the Security Service, got a nod to continue. "Be aware that their influence isn't just in the UK and Albania though. They have strong networks all over Europe, in the US, China, the Middle East, even down in Australia. They are a force to be reckoned with, have ties in Italy with the Cosa Nostra, the Sacra Corona Unita, the Camorra, the Società Foggiana – I could go on, but I think you've all got the gist of it. They are connected, they are strong. They are also brutal, as bad as any terrorist organisation on the planet." She paused, giving others a chance to speak. No-one bothered.

"We are all aware that of late they have been targeting our police force, intentionally killing officers, planned hits, not just unlucky gunfights during a robbery that's got out of hand. They are trying to terrify our people, stopping them from carrying out their duties effectively."

"We need to send extra people to scenes of crimes and reported incidents," Dan Griffin added. "Sending a patrol out alone is just not safe anymore. That's tying up resources."

Janet nodded. "In the eyes of both MI6 and MI5, they are now representing a threat to the running of the UK as a whole," she said. "To this end we want to consider them not as a criminal gang, but as a terrorist organisation."

"And that gives us more scope in what we can do to combat them," Mary Kemp added. "And that's the reason that we are all here in Hereford today." She smiled, a lady of few words. "Inspector Griffin, you will be attached to 22nd SAS Regiment for the foreseeable future, working directly with Colonel Green here. We'd like you to start outlining what you think we should do to eliminate our Albanian problem, and then to work here with the colonel to prepare a plan to execute those ideas."

Janet grinned at the two men. "Sounds simple, doesn't it?"

"Piece of piss," Alex allowed, sighing. "Okay Dan, the stage is yours. I'll just try and make up answers as we go along."

"So how did it go?"

Janet was driving her BMW back towards London, the traffic already thinning at six-thirty, Hereford well off to her rear. "Not bad Ruth," she replied to her handsfree. "We've set an incredibly high bar once again, and now we leave it to our super trooper to invent a solution." There was a chuckle from the other end of the phone.

"Is there anything I need to do? Resources? Funding?" the PM asked after a second or two.

"Not yet," the spy boss responded. "We had a great brainstorming session, left everyone with something to do. Mary and myself have to see what assets we can use on the ground, get them to identify targets. We don't wait for a special occasion, we just ID, check as best we can, then hit them."

"Could end up with collateral damage," Ruth Maybank grumbled. "It's a little loose, isn't it?"

"It'll be the same as we do with terror suspects," Janet replied. "We do everything in our power to check things, plus call in our feeds from GCHQ, Interpol, and all of the rest. If it looks bad, we stop it."

"And how did the partnership appear to go?"

"Dan's a fairly down to earth guy, and we know Alex is the same. After hearing some of the details of the hits the mafia boys have made on the police, Alex was all for going in all guns blazing, but Dan reminded him that the police are going to have to pick up the pieces one day, and probably still without having a weapon." Janet slowed as she saw traffic building up ahead. The M25 wasn't far away, London's biggest carpark. "I felt the same as Alex, but Dan helped keep things grounded. I think Mary was happier with that than I was."

"You two have been too close for too long," Ruth said. "You can probably telepath messages to one another."

"You might be right," Janet conceded. "How do you want to play this? I give you a weekly update, plus prewarning of anything about to go down?"

The Prime Minister considered the options, staring out of her Number Ten's flat window. "That might upset Mary, putting you as the conduit. Why not use the old tested system and put Mike in loop? You'll no doubt tell him anyway." Mike Sanders, Alex's ex-boss, now Janet's lover, and another soldier that the PM had a great affection for. A neutral but not quite.

"It's an idea," Janet allowed. "And with his background, he might even flag up something that the rest of us miss."

"And he's safe. No unwanted chatter from Mike."

"I'll ask him this evening, but I can already guess the answer. Any excuse to work with his protege again."

Ruth laughed. "Apples from the same bunch," she chortled. "Some things will never change."

Just a week later, a dead body was found beside a giant bottle bin outside of a Soho nightclub. It was beaten, tortured, fingers had been removed with the assistance of bolt croppers, teeth with pliers. Burn marks scarred the chest and genitals. Wrists and ankles showed that the man had been manacled to some solid immobile object, probably in an upright position.

He had a bald head, a goatee beard, a string of coloured beads holding it together.

Externally, the Metropolitan Police kept it tight, didn't release the fact that he was one of their own to the media, just that a man had been found dead and that they suspected that he had been involved in drugs, a turf war of some sort between rival gangs.

Internally, alarm bells were ringing loudly. Another of their number had been murdered, and that same person had been involved with a missing Nigerian bouncer, a man who had disappeared from the face of the earth after a failed club raid just over a week earlier.

It didn't take much to join the dots.

The Albanians had struck again.

Preparing For The Worst

Dan Griffin was waiting outside of Alex Green's office at seven in the morning, the SAS colonel an early starter himself but still beaten. It wasn't their normal routine, the police officer usually letting Alex have a couple of hours to focus on other matters first, allowing him time to catch up with his team back in London. Out of office he might be, out of touch he wasn't.

"Morning Dan," Alex greeted him, unlocking the office door. "Did I forget something?"

Dan pushed the door closed, put a printout on the soldier's desk. It was headed 'For Internal Use Only – STRICTLY CONFIDENTIAL' and had the Yard's logo embossed on the paper. "Read that, then I'll explain."

It was only half a page of words, just three paragraphs. It referred to the death of an undercover police constable, gave a summary of his injuries. Alex read it swiftly. "Sounds terrible," he concluded. "Some bloody warped bastards out there, that's for sure."

"It was the Albanians," Dan replied. "This man had a contact, someone working in one of their clubs. The contact was a bouncer – a Nigerian – and he can't be located. In all probability, he's in the same shape as this poor bugger. Dead."

Alex nodded, letting Dan speak.

"The bouncer tipped the copper off about a major drugs delivery to the club. We arranged a hit, hoped to catch them in the act. I was on that raid. We got nothing – they set us up, dragged us in to identify their snitch." He sighed. "In effect, we pointed the Albanians to their target, revealed their weakness. We got those men killed."

Alex hesitated, knowing how it felt to be responsible for the death of good men, an occupational hazard with his job. Things went wrong in times of high stress, and it was often a fine line between winning a battle and losing it. Good people got hurt. "You were doing your job Dan," he offered, trying to support the man. "You – and your team – were working on a tip-off, and if t had gone well, you'd all have been having a beer on it. This time it didn't."

Dan was an Inspector, knew the risks, understood the job, but right now he just felt horribly low. "These people are beating us, Alex," he murmured. "They are taking the piss, playing with us."

The SAS man could see that he was right, but this wasn't a time to agree. "And that's why we have to come up with a plan that takes them down a peg or two," he said. "It's on us to make things change, avenge all of the people that have suffered."

Dan nodded, taking a deep breath. He knew that it was time to move on.

Alex watched as the policeman left his office, heading for his own private space. He'd no doubt go over the failed raid, analyse what he could have done better, how he could have stopped what had just happened.

Fallout was coming. Fallout from a stressed out policeman, and a soldier determined to assist him. And political fallout too.

It was another member of the thin blue line that had fallen, but the timing meant that this single death would become much larger, representative of all the other recent killings of the protectors of the peace by the Albanian Mafia.

People in high places would soon be baying for blood. Demanding results.

Alex waited for the call.

Luan Shehu also waited, but not for a call.

He knew what Dren and his boys had done to the undercover cop, had ordered it himself, but now he was having doubts. Targeting the police was one thing, and the filth didn't seem to have an answer to that. Sure, they made televised statements, threatened and paraded, but in the end they were governed by the law of the land. Their options were limited. They needed to catch his men in the act, have enough evidence to prosecute them, and they had to do it in a way that would stand up to the scrutiny of the legal justice system. Entrapment was out, shooting first and asking questions later was alien to them.

It was much easier being a criminal he thought with a quiet smile.

But taking one of their own, torturing the man, putting him out on the streets like some sort of a trophy... Had they gone too far? Would it trigger a reaction that none of them had imagined?

If someone took out one of his people and made an example of them, the response would be instantaneous. He would identify the rival, take them down with maximum force. He would need to prove to everyone who the alpha male was, the main man, the head honcho. Failing to do that would lose him not just his face, but his business. Losing your dominance meant losing your patch.

He had his contacts within the police force, people on whom he had secrets that they didn't want out there, or where he had found their price. Everyone had a price.

It was time to find out what rumours were circulating.

"Are things ready to go Mike?" Ruth Maybank asked, totally missing out on the pleasantries.

Mike Sanders considered raising that point, decided that the stress in the Prime Minister's voice suggested that he shouldn't. The lady didn't sound to be in a great place.

"I'm assuming you mean with the new Alex venture?" he replied, buying a little time. It just might be enough to calm things down a notch.

"Of course."

He could hear Ruth sigh, guessed that she was realising that her approach was maybe a little impolite.

"Alex's team are always ready, Ruth," he said after a second. "They just need a target, a mission to fulfil. We're missing that target right now, but I know that Janet and Mary are both using their secret squirrels to try and find one. Should have something soon."

"I need something now," the PM replied, her voice a little softer now. "You're aware that another policeman has been killed?"

"I heard from Alex, who heard from Dan. I haven't seen the details, but I hear that it wasn't very pleasant."

"Understatement," the lady responded. "And people are starting to get a little excited. We need to lay down a marker, show these scumbags that they cannot do this sort of thing. What do you think about publicly announcing that the SAS will be involved? It might pacify a few people."

Mike stared at the screen of his phone for a second, wondered how best to answer. Revealing that the government were going to step up the fight against the Albanians would certainly take some of the heat off the PM, but advising the bad guys that the SAS were on their backs wasn't great for Alex. "I think that should be kept quiet for now," he finally replied. "Surprise is a weapon, and I'm sure that Alex would prefer it in his arsenal."

He could hear the PM release a pent up breath, imagined her having her eyes tightly shut, another plan destroyed. "I understand," she whispered.

"Let me talk to Janet, convey the situation to her," he said. "Perhaps one of the agencies has something ready to go." He knew it wasn't enough but going off half-cocked just got people hurt. "If they have something, then Alex will make a plan, complete any specialist training needed, and he'll be ready to rock and roll." He knew it sounded crude, but that was what he felt Ruth needed right now.

"Give me a call later," the PM said, her voice more like normal now. "I need something, and very soon."

Alex had toured the facilities in Stirling Lines with Dan, tried to explain to him what made the SAS different from other troops all around the world. He'd allowed him to take part in a Killing Rooms session, sitting in as a hostage; had him try a part of the Selection – a run with only a lightweight pack in the Brecons with some of his boys; showed him close quarter battle training out at Pontrilas, plus the aircraft and railway hostage simulation mock-ups close by. It was easier to understand the elite soldiers limitations if you understood their capabilities.

Today, Alex thought that Dan needed a different approach. The man was quiet and introverted, still blaming himself for what had happened to the undercover policeman. He needed reminding that their jobs were not always about good news.

They walked through the barracks, and Alex led the way to a clocktower, seemingly out of place on the edge of the parade ground.

"See the names on there?" he said pointing.

Dan nodded, unsure what they were doing there. "Those are the people who died on duty, isn't it?" he asked.

"So you've done your homework," Alex replied with a wry grin. "And yes, that's right. They failed to 'beat the clock' in our lingo." He gave the tower a small nod of respect, wondered not for the first time if he'd ever be a part of it. "They were all doing their jobs, often under the most unforgiving of circumstances. They died all over the world, in conflicts that normal people will probably never get to know about."

"I'd heard about it," the policeman replied. "It's pretty humbling," he added.

"None of them wanted to die," Alex went on. "But it was why they joined, what they believed in. They passed the toughest course in the military world to be in those shit places, fighting against odds that were simply impossible. And if we could ask them, I'm certain that every one of them would say they'd do it all again."

Dan looked at him, getting the message.

"Your man was doing what he did because he believed in it. What happened to him was dreadful, but we will put that right. Soon."

Alex just didn't realise how soon.

They met in an inconspicuous café off the Embankment, somewhere easy enough for all of them to get to. Janet ordered a tall latte, Mary a mocha, and Mike Sanders settled on an Evian water. He'd called the meeting.

"We need a target," he told the other two. "Ruth called me. She's under pressure following the murder of the undercover cop." It was explanation enough.

"If we rush things, we'll end up with more of our covert people dead," Mary complained.

Mike nodded, fully understanding the knife edge that the secret operators lived on. Press too hard, and you exposed yourself. And being undercover usually meant no support, no back-up. Exposure was fatal.

"We have some names," Mary continued. "Ninety percenters, but not certainties. Definitely involved with the mafia gangs, but perhaps not the leaders."

"And we'd like to take them down from the top," Janet added. "Cut off the serpents head before it knows we are on to them."

"Exactly," the MI5 leader said. "Once we show our hands, a second strike will be more difficult. Surprise will be gone. Drawbridges will be raised. You understand."

Mike nodded. He got it. Shock was a great weapon. "I got the feeling that Ruth needs something now," he told them. "I can only guess that it's political pressure, but who knows. We all know about the dirty tricks that go on within our wonderful corridors of power. It could be any number of things."

"It's public confidence," Janet said with a sigh. "That's my read. If the police can't defend themselves, then how can they help Joe Public? Ruth sort of hinted at it recently, said something about public confidence being low. I think that's the demon that she's dealing with."

"Added to the usual pressures from the opposition party, who doubtless will be making a meal of it all," Mary added.

Mike sipped his water, put down the glass. "We're drifting off subject," he reminded them. "Can the two of you put your heads together, give me a date when you'll be ready. We need action, and we need it ASAP."

The two spymasters nodded. Mike was right, even if he was not their chief.

Janet finished her coffee, started to stand. "We'll offer some sort of a proposal by the end of today," she said.

The MI5 boss also stood, nodded her agreement.

"I'll let Ruth know." Mike knew it wasn't the answer that the PM wanted, but it was better than none. Wheels were turning.

"How quickly can you put something together?"

Mike had called Alex as soon as he left the two spy chiefs, more to give him a heads-up than to pressure him. He knew that the SAS would be ready to go at the drop of a hat, always had people on standby.

"How long's a piece of string?" Alex replied. "You know that we always have a team ready, but until we know the target, I can't make a plan."

Mike pursed his lips, knowing that Alex was correct. "I guess I just want you to know things are going to happen soon," he said. "Ruth is under pressure, and Janet and Mary have promised to come up with a proposal by close of play today."

"Appreciated," the SAS colonel allowed, aware that Mike knew better than most what his team could do. "I'll be waiting."

"As soon as I hear anything, then you will too."

Ready To Go

"Dren Sula runs a club in the West End called the Blue Beaver. Lap dancing, prostitution, a small scale drugs operation if we're not wrong, people trafficking, girls especially. All the normal shit – promised a great job, then forced to sell their bodies. Do enough tricks and you'll get your passport back. Nothing out of the ordinary."

Ruth Maybank, Janet Anderson, and Mike Sanders listened intently as Mary Kemp made her presentation. "We believe he may be the head of Albanian operations here in the capital, and if he isn't, he's not far off the top. He has strong connections back home too, his family all coming from the Tirana area, some links to senior politicians there."

"So he's probably the top dog over here," Ruth said, checking that she'd understood things right. "So why don't we just pull him in?"

"I thought that you wanted to make a statement, show these people who's the boss. If we just pull him in, they'll lawyer him up and take us to the cleaners," Mary replied. "We have nothing concrete on him. One of our people knows someone down the chain a bit, and they said that Sula is a top man. You wanted something fast. It's the best I can give you without more time to get deeper into them."

"Our people confirm that the Sula clan are big over the water. Strong ties to the Italian mafia too," Janet confirmed. "He's definitely a somebody."

"So taking him down would shake-up the locals at least," Mike said. "But how do we do it legally? And how do we handle it without getting normal people in the line of fire?"

"We can't have a friendly fire incident," Ruth agreed. "But we do need something to show that we are in control, not the bad guys."

"Can we draw them out? Tempt them with something?"

"We could pose as a rival gang, make it a turf issue," Janet said. "But all of this takes time, and you wanted action fast. I think we just get Alex to raid the club, drag in all of the group. Maybe one of them will talk, grass up the rest of them."

Ruth looked uncomfortable. "I want to reassure the public, but I don't want to appear to be breaking the rules. It's got to be clean."

Janet glanced at Mary, aware that the PM was asking too much.

"We can't just sit on the fence Ruth," she said, her lengthy relationship with the Prime Minister allowing her to be so forward. "Going in half-cocked will get someone hurt."

Ruth pulled at her lower lip, out of her comfort zone. "Then perhaps we shouldn't do anything before you've had more time to look into things," she suggested. "Do it properly."

"Let's put the facts we know on the table," Mike said, his soldier's mind finding order where there was little of it. "This Sula bloke is Albanian. He has ties to the mafia, both Albanian and Italian. He is involved in prostitution, people trafficking, and possibly drugs. He is certainly a criminal."

Mary nodded. "Without any doubt."

"Then why don't we do this," the ex-SAS colonel continued. "You talk to your people and try and get a bit more from their sources. I talk to Alex and get him to move a team up to London. Maybe if he gives this Blue Beaver place a once over he'll see a way to move us forward."

Ruth nodded, happy to stall for a little more time. "Can we meet again tomorrow? Perhaps late afternoon?"

"That gives me time to get Alex with us," Mike agreed. "And he's the man who has to make it happen."

Luan Shehu had one of those feelings again, a sixth sense telling him that something was simply not right. He'd been having doubts since they'd killed off the undercover agent, something constantly nagging at the back of his brain. He couldn't quite place what it was, best described it as a sort of unreachable itch somewhere deep in his skull.

"It's too quiet," he told himself. That was the best he could do to sum it up.

None of his operations were reporting any police problems. In his line of work, that wasn't normal. No matter how watertight you kept your operation, when you were involved in so many 'dodgy' activities, you expected some interference from the authorities. As it was, he hadn't had a reported raid on any of his clubs since the one on the Blue Beaver. None of his hookers had been pulled for soliciting. And Border Force seemed to have backed off on the people smuggling operations, the overloaded dinghies coming to the British coast without any intervention.

It just wasn't normal.

Shehu had a number of contacts in the authorities, people who had costly habits, or secrets they'd prefer to keep that way. It was time to use a few of them, to see what was going down.

Because something was. Had to be.

"So they want a team up here, preferably today," Mike explained to the man in Hereford. "Standby only right now, but I can't see it staying that way for too long."

"I'll send up the anti-terrorist standby unit today, have them with you this evening," the SAS colonel said. "A couple of them can run eyes over the prospective target, check out the lay of the land."

"Ruth would like you to join tomorrow's meeting, if possible have a look at the club yourself."

Alex sighed. As boss of the regiment, he tried to keep his hands off things, let his soldiers have space to develop their own ideas. He wasn't averse to adding his own take on the eventual plan, but delegation was key to bettering his team. He wouldn't be in the driving seat forever. "I need to be home tonight," he told his friend. They'd worked together for many years now, seen good and bad times. "It's young Alex's ninth birthday. I have to be there."

"Understood," Mike replied. "I'll sort out some accommodation for the boys, just let me have numbers. Then we see you tomorrow morning."

Alex nodded to himself. Andile wasn't going to be so happy.

His sources in the police had nothing to offer that explained the standoff, promised to keep their ears to the ground.

"I think that the way the undercover man was taken out has riled some of the top brass," one of them offered. "They seem to be having a lot of 'closed doors' meetings, often not in our offices."

Shehu decided to press a politician with a taste for the ladies, one that he had some rather explicit pictures of. "I know that there have been some meetings between the PM and our intelligence community," the man offered. "But it seems that nothing was recorded during those get togethers. It's all very off the record," he added.

"Do some digging," the mafia boss ordered. "I need to know more."

The little information that was coming out did nothing to settle his suspicions. Something was going on, and he had to know what it was, and fast. If he was correct, the authorities were planning something that was going to have a serious influence on his operations.

Luan Shehu hadn't survived this long by being a step behind.

"The Met want to be in on it," Ruth said, addressing the meeting. "I had an audience with the Commissioner this morning, and he thinks we should keep the SAS in a supporting role only," she added.

"So no need for me to be here," Alex said, wondering why he'd bothered with such an early start. He'd left his home in Hereford at six. "You have my team here, they just tag along on the police raid, sit it out in a covert furniture van while the boys in blue grab the fame and glory."

Mike held up a hand, stopping the irritated colonel. "On this occasion, I agree with Alex. If the troopers aren't leading, then there's little need for them to be there. All we're doing is the same as the last time."

Ruth looked frustrated. "I'm just trying to keep everyone happy," she said. "Marginalizing the police makes them look weak. That's no good for anyone."

"They raided that club just a week back," Alex informed them all. Janet and Mary looked up at that, until now happy to keep out of the conversation. They'd done their bit, brought in the intel. "Dan Griffin was on the team leading the drug search. They found nothing, ended up with a missing bouncer and a dead undercover cop."

A silence descended on the room. This was new to them all, information that the Metropolitan Police had withheld from the PM.

"According to Dan, it was as if this Sula character had been expecting it," Alex added. "The place was clean, too clean. Dan thinks that there must be someone passing inside info to the Albanians."

"We should postpone," Janet said. "We need more intel."

"Then we look weak," the head of MI5 replied, an unhappy expression on her face. "We're being reactive, not proactive."

Ruth knew that she needed to make a decision, reassert her authority. She was the Prime Minister. "The Commissioner was anxious to get things moving," she said. "The police need to appear in command, to have the criminals on the back foot. We need to turn over the club, and we need the police to lead that raid."

Alex shrugged his shoulders, not really wanting to add more. "Tell me when, tell me how many soldiers you want in support, and I'll do my thing."

The PM nodded, not at all happy with the outcome, but pleased to have at least some sort of reluctant support. "Tomorrow," she said decisively. "And I'd like you to be on hand Alex," she added.

Another shrug of the shoulders, the SAS colonel showing little emotion. "I'm here," he said. "I can also sit this one out in the covert furniture van," he added with a grin. "Just one thing though: let's keep my guys right off the radar. No mention to anyone. Surprise is everything."

The remark raised tight smiles from all at the briefing. The pressures on the PM were clear, the result of the meeting not quite what any of them had hoped for.

All that they were doing was putting the boys in blue in harm's way once more. The only difference was that they now believed that there was a leak somewhere in their system, someone that might just allow the information to get out to the gangs once again. Perhaps with mortal consequences.

"Tomorrow it is then," Mike confirmed, scanning the faces of everyone present to ensure understanding. "Please get the Met to liaise with Alex for their requirements," he added, addressing the PM. "Unless you want me to take it up with them?"

Ruth nodded silently, understanding that no-one really bought in to the outcome. "Please Mike," she said. One less thing to be laid at her door.

"There's going to be a raid on one of your clubs tomorrow night, that one in Soho, the Blue Beaver," the police informer told Shehu.

"Again?" the Albanian asked, a little surprised. "It was searched only about a week back," he added. Had the man mixed things up? Twice in a week?

"They are hoping to pull in the manager, some bloke called Sula, or something like that."

The name was right, and perhaps the authorities had got wind about who had killed their operative, planned to get the people behind it. "So the police will target the Beaver," Shehu said to himself.

"That's the word on the ground," the copper said. "So, I've done my bit. How about a nice young Romanian virgin by way of payment?"

When Dan Griffin heard from Alex about the planned hit on the Blue Beaver he immediately contacted his Chief Inspector, volunteering to join the operation. It made sense: he'd been a part of the last visit, he knew the layout of the place and where to go to corner their target. It would also help him assuage his guilt for the loss of the undercover agent, something that he still felt had been a direct result of that raid.

It came as a shock when his request was turned down.

"I was there, I've met this Sula bloke, I should be a part of this," he stormed to the SAS man.

Alex let the anger wash away, well aware that Dan felt some degree of ownership for the previous failed venture. At the end of the day, he also wasn't too happy with the way decisions were going. His SAS team should either be doing what they did best or keeping well away from it all. Right now, he felt that they were doing neither, just stuck somewhere in the middle, a 'just in case' back-up.

"You can come and sit in with my team if it helps," he finally offered. "We'll have comms with the police, see camera footage as they go in."

It wasn't what the police inspector wanted, but it was certainly better than just being frozen out altogether. "Appreciated," he sighed. At least he'd still be in the loop.

"You can get bored and drink tea with the SAS team in a freezing covert truck," Alex added with a grin. "And you can keep me company too."

Dan almost smiled, his anger fading. If this secondment had taught him one thing, it was that these elite soldiers wouldn't be getting upset about being a little uncomfortable for an hour or two. After what they went through just to get into the unit, freezing your nuts off just wasn't a problem.

"I'll bring the biscuits," he offered.

Alex grinned. "A man after my own heart."

Action!

"Hello Trojan Support, this is Trojan One. We're ready to go. Comms check."

Dan Griffin could imagine the police team leader waiting in the shadows, his men poised for their big entrance, firearms into the shoulder, half hoping that they might get to use them, the rest dreading the thought. It wasn't so much the fear of needing to use excessive force that they were concerned about, more about the form filling and red tape that would follow if they even discharged their weapons. It was only just over a week since Dan had been in just the same position, in exactly the same location. He could feel the tension.

"Receiving you loud and clear," the SAS radio man acknowledged, each soldier wired for sound, each nodding to confirm his system was operable. "We're in position."

Alex glanced around his men, each kitted out all in black, Kevlar vests already strapped tight. Their weapons were close to hand, MP5s chosen for the close confines of the building. They'd decided that a team of four should suffice, their expectations of seeing any action low. Dan Griffin and the radio operator would remain with the vehicle if they were called on, the link between the police and military units.

"We're going in now," Trojan One broadcast. "Bodycams are on, you should have the feed."

"We have the visual."

The six men in the British Telecom liveried van all watched the screens, followed the Trojan crew as they moved swiftly up to the main door of the club, the pictures a little jerky, unstable.

"Take out the door," the policeman ordered, one of the team slamming a small battering ram into the area of the lock. Wood splintered, a shoulder charge finishing the job, and the team were in.

"There's no bouncers," Dan muttered, mainly to himself.

Alex checked the television screen, confirming the police inspectors observation. "And there were last time?" he asked.

"Just where they are now."

The SAS man was just about to grab the radio, to warn the police that something seemed to be off. He was halfway across the van when the picture from the team leader's camera flipped upwards, no longer focussing on the way ahead of him.

Dren Sula gave the signal, and eight men leapt up from behind various pieces of furniture and the wooden serving area of the bar, all armed with automatic weapons, all of them ready to lay down fire.

The leading copper took a burst to his chest, smashing him into reverse, the body armour saving his life, even if it didn't feel that way right now.

"We're under fire!" he grunted into his radio, something that was totally unnecessary. The racket could be heard outside of the Blue Beaver, even through the padded walls of the BT van.

Shots were still hammering out, the confines of the bar area echoing with them, deafening both the coppers and the mafia gang members. Police were trying to find any type of cover, crawling back the way they'd come in, trying to get a wall between themselves and the Albanian crew. It was pandemonium, the airwaves a confused blather of conversations and curses, control totally gone.

Sula got up, the police on the run. It was time to get out there, to finish them off. It was the end for the club, but it was another victory for the criminals. The information Shehu had received meant that they were ready, that the law were again left wanting. He waved to his men, encouraged them to move forward after the retreating authorities.

Alex and his team of three were out of the vehicle, weapons at the ready, heading towards the main door of the club, the only entry point on this side of the building.

"Watch out for friendly fire," he warned. "They will be coming out this way too."

As if in confirmation, a police officer fell through the front entrance, a second just behind him. That left four unaccounted for, still inside. There was no time to think, just time to get inside and save the men.

Dan appeared beside Alex, anxious to get involved.

"Keep your people out of the way," Alex ordered, slightly annoyed to find the man there. "We're going in, but it has to be fast. Just my men."

The first SAS man was in the doorway now, pressed against the wall, a colleague already passing by him, weapon sweeping arcs in front of him. Another policeman staggered towards him, stunned but apparently uninjured, the trooper quickly grabbing his shoulder, pushing him back towards the door.

"Where are the rest?"

The man pointed behind him, clearly shaken. "The bar area," he shouted, trying to be heard above the racket of gunshots. "The skipper's been hit."

Alex pointed to where the main noise was coming from. There was no time to assess the situation, not if they wanted to save the other officers. "Flashbangs!" he said into the throat microphone.

The lead trooper pulled one out, his man in support following suit. They threw the grenades through the half-open doorway, knowing they'd be equally bad for both the Albanians and the police team, but that they wouldn't be fatal. They waited, eyes closed, ears waiting for the shockwave. A flash, a pause in the shooting, and the SAS men were in the bar, searching for threats.

A policeman lay beside a raised dancing area, trying to use a dance pole to get to his feet. Two others lay unmoving closer to the bar, their uniforms identifying them from the enemy.

Alex was also in the bar now, hunting for targets, seeing that some of the Albanians were already recovering from the stunningly bright explosions. One was raising a weapon, firing as he did so, still not quite with it, but dangerous all the same. Alex took him down, a short burst from his H & K, moving on to the next threat.

To his left, another soldier fired several rounds, taking out another of the criminals. Others were getting to their feet, rubbing their eyes, some trying to continue the fight, some clearly surrendering.

"Put down your weapons!" Alex ordered, hoping that the words would be heard after the cacophony of noise.

One of the men followed his order, three others did the opposite, raising their assortment of handguns and machine pistols, trying to continue taking the fight to the soldiers. More bursts of fire, really just rattles from the MP5s, the SAS men removing the danger. For them, this was hours of training in the Killing Rooms put into practice. Almost automatic.

And then there was silence, just the sound of boots on broken glass and the smell of a gun battle laced with fear.

"Check the bodies," Alex said. "We want no surprises."

The SAS team moved from man to man, checking that they were not going to become a threat. Six dead, one from the initial police entrance, the rest from the soldiers. Two alive, the one that surrendered and the other wounded. Both were secured with PlastiCuffs, moved out of the building.

Two of the police officers were wounded, one unable to walk unassisted. They were transferred outside to a waiting ambulance. One of the team wasn't so lucky.

Alex knew that if the SAS team had led the raid, the outcome would have been different. Entry wouldn't have been as obvious as the front door, the ambush undone from the outset.

It didn't make him feel any better. Hindsight was always twenty/twenty vision.

In the harsh LED lighting that the team had turned on, the club looked cheap and tacky, the dive that it was. Blood now spattered the walls, stray bullets holed masonry and furniture. This job was over.

Luan Shehu got the call from Tirana only twenty-five minutes after the action was over, still unsure of the outcome himself, no call from his head man so far.

"Sula is dead," a voice told him. "Shot by the police."

It was tempting to ask where the information had come from, to see how a senior mafia family in Albania could know how things had gone at the Blue Beaver faster than the head of their British operation here in London. He knew better than to ask, to keep quiet, save face. Dren Sula had good connections back in the motherland. Or he did have.

"I'm looking into to it right now," he replied, a bare faced lie, but the best he could think of. The man was no doubt right. Sula had failed to contact him. It could only mean one thing.

"Find out how it happened and put it right."

The phone went dead. Shehu let out a long sigh. Something had failed tonight, and it shouldn't have. He had been prewarned of the raid, even knew the planned timing of it. His team were well armed, professional fighters. They should have won the game, hands down. His intel had been flawed, something not right.

He set down the landline, picked up a burner phone and pressed the only number on it. It was time to get his police informant to start digging. Maybe for the last time in his life. That man's days were horribly numbered.

"It was kept very quiet, really just the upper echelons involved in the planning," the policeman told him. "Everyone I've asked knew nothing about it. But like I said, there was a SAS team in support – Special Air Service," the man clarified, trying to rebuild bridges.

"I know who the SAS are," Shehu replied, his voice flat, trying hard to hide his anger. He lifted his glass of whisky, saluted the man opposite him. "Anything else?"

"The police lost one man, two injured," the informer said, hoping that this would help offset things slightly. "Oh, and the SAS team was led by that headline grabber, Alex Green. He always seems to be in the thick of things. You know who I mean?"

The mafia boss did know of the soldier – who didn't in the UK? He'd been involved in the cure for COVID, had stopped a return to The Troubles in Northern Ireland, had saved the rhinoceros in Southern Africa, recently been involved in stopping a nuclear war in the Middle East. "I know of him, but I have never seen him," he allowed.

"I can see if we have any photos on file," the policeman offered, feeling on higher ground now. "He tends to keep a very low profile."

"He has a family," Shehu said softly. He also knew that the man's wife was the doctor behind the COVID vaccine, a South African if he recalled. "Do you have any details of the family?"

The lawman knew that he now had a purpose, a reason not to be punished – yet. "I'll get straight on to it," he replied. "I believe that they live in Hereford but give me a couple of hours."

Shehu nodded. Nothing hurt a man more than removing his nearest and dearest. Nothing was more torturous.

"You have until midnight."

The Unthinkable

"That was your team last night?" Andile asked when Alex finally found time to call her. He'd been caught up in paperwork and report writing most of the night, eventually getting about four hours of sleep at three in the morning.

"I don't think I need to answer that one," he replied, a grin on his face. Andile understood enough to know that operations were generally carried out on the QT, that admitting to things on an open phone line was far from best practice.

"I'll take that as a maybe," the doctor responded. "Are you home tonight?"

Alex rubbed his eyes, knowing that what he had to say wasn't going to be well received. It was Friday morning, the weekend looming. "They want us up here for a few more days," he said. "A few other things to sort out."

Andile sighed, knowing that moaning wouldn't help. "I was hoping to get away to Bristol for a night with the kids. New school term and all that. Uniforms, sports kit, all the usual."

"Do it," the SAS man replied immediately. "It's only an hour and a half's drive. Gives you a chance to get something new for yourself too." He wished he could offer to meet up there but knew that it was too soon to be able to do so. Though the Met had lost an officer, they had won a major battle with the Albanians. Senior police officers wanted to continue that motion, score some more points with the public, disrupt the gangs a bit more. "And a night in a hotel will be good for all of you. Pick one with a pool."

"And you'll pick up the tab?" the South African lady asked, a cheeky lilt in her voice.

Alex considered it was a fair cost for being away once again.

One day it would all be over.

Finding personal details of members of Britain's special forces wasn't as hard as one might think, but Alex Green had been careful to keep a low profile despite his exploits. For his wife, this wasn't so simple. As Head of Research and Innovation at Hereford County Hospital and the force behind the COVID vaccine, she was often used to present new ideas and developments to the international community through contributions to medical journals, occasionally making it on to local television and radio. It meant that images of her were easy to access, even without the use of the police computer.

Luan Shehu arranged surveillance on her place of work, followed her car home with ease, and now knew the Green's home address. And that they had two children, a boy, and a girl.

"There's no sign of the soldier?" he asked the man watching the property.

"Just the woman and the two children."

Shehu considered his options. Taking them hostage was high on his list, but not knowing where the SAS colonel was meant this could be risky. Did he carry a weapon at home? Did he have panic alarms in the property, something that would bring the weight of the garrison down on his people if triggered? There was just too much he was uncertain of.

"Watch them," he said. "See if the kids come out. Talk to them." Adults were good at keeping secrets, even under duress. Children often spoke first and thought later. "Try and see what their plans are for the weekend. There might be an opportunity."

"We have another lead, an operation over in Southend. Supposedly, the Albanian's headquarters for drugs here in England."

"Where is the intelligence from?" Alex asked, always trying to get a second opinion on things. "I mean, that last operation was obviously leaked, the police team ambushed. There were no punters, no Toms, just the shooters waiting for the police team to enter. If we'd not been there..." He let his words hang.

Mary Kemp grimaced. "It's like all our intel," she finally offered. "It's very rarely a hundred percent. But it's good, checks out," she added.

Alex nodded. His team were really just the hammer, the people who put the nails in the coffins of the bad guys. They were there to do the bidding of the government of the day, whether it was driven by the intelligence community for home or abroad. "When?"

"Tomorrow," the Deputy Commissioner replied. "Before word has a chance to get out again. We are keeping a lid on things, but we also want things to be police led again."

The SAS colonel inhaled a long breath, thinking about how to respond. "I'd prefer that we led, but then your team come in at the end and take the glory. Below radar is always the best for us," he finally offered.

"I'm afraid you're on standby again," the senior policeman said. "No discussions. I have the PM's support on this."

Janet Anderson discretely gave a nod, letting Alex know that she'd sounded out Ruth Maybank. As the policeman had said, no discussions.

"Let me have the details and I'll organise my team. But hear me out – I have a way to support you better but in a way that the boys in blue still lead." At least on the surface, Alex thought to himself.

The Albanian could see the football occasionally rising above the garden fence, disappearing from view after the skywards loop. The kids were outside, but also out of view. He waited, sometimes spotting the black woman at one of the windows, looking out expectantly. Someone was due to arrive. The SAS soldier, or a friend?

The question was answered quarter of an hour later, a small Toyota pulling up on to the drive, a woman and a small girl climbing out, the door of the house opening, a little girl running out of it. He watched as the two girls hugged, then the target appearing at the door, greeting the other lady.

Friends, the watcher surmised. Would this give him the break that he wanted?

Initially everyone disappeared into the house, the door shutting behind them. A false alarm, no opportunity to exploit.

It was around ten minutes later that the two girls left the building, the black one carrying the football he'd seen earlier. He guessed that they were around five years of age, happy to escape the boring adults. He wound down his window, hoping for a chance to speak to them, to gain some sort of a lead. His car was over thirty metres distant, too far to follow their conversation.

Getting out and walking over to the children would cause the neighbours to notice him, perhaps cause the girls mothers to report the vehicle. He needed to be patient.

It took another twenty minutes for an opportunity to present itself.

The girls ran around the front lawn, chasing the ball, kicking it off the house walls. It bounced towards his car, got wedged under the front bumper. Cautiously, the two youngsters approached the car, uncertain if they were in trouble.

He considered getting out, decided that this might scare them off, waited.

"Can we get the ball out?" the black kid asked, almost at the window.

"Of course," he said, a friendly smile plastered on his lips. "Just be a little more careful," he added. "You don't want to break a window, do you?"

The girl nodded her agreement, went to the front of the car, her friend following. He could hear the second youth saying something about stopping playing, maybe just sitting down, having a chat. He sensed that the chance might be going but decided to hold his position.

"Thanks," the first child said, showing him the ball. The two of them moved away, sat down on the lawn beside the house, now just fifteen metres distant.

"So what are you doing this weekend?" the second girl asked. "We're going to the pictures."

The Albanian smiled to himself. Everything comes to those who wait.

The police strike team were ready just off Journeyman's Way on Temple Farm Industrial Estate, the team in two unmarked cars, waiting to go. They'd taken the simple route in.

Alex and his team had walked in, their vehicles dropping them off at Southend Airport, two teams of four men each, one heading for the target's rear wall, the other to be on hand close to the front entrance. The industrial unit itself was small, a roller door to one side of the main entrance, the walls a cheap looking grey corrugated aluminium. It didn't look like the Albanian Mafia's main HQ for drugs coming into the UK, but all of the intelligence services were in agreement that it was.

It was coming up to eight in the evening, the other premises on the estate dark and deserted. A light shone inside of the target. No movement was visible, no vehicles present.

"Probably just a security light," one of the police team offered.

"It looks more like the sort of place you'd take the car to have your tyres done than a drug den," another added.

"We're in position," Alex said over the radio. "I'm at the back. There's no doors, but we can blow out a section of wall, come in that way."

"We're in the park just off Sumpters Way," the head of the second SAS team added in everyone's headsets. "Ready to go if needed."

"If Trojan is ready, then I'll send a man forward to prepare our entry point," Alex informed them all. "When we blow the wall out, that will be the signal for you to go. We'll be in already, so watch out for blue-on-blue." Doing it this way made the police appear to be the lead team, but in truth it meant that the SAS team would be in first, the area hopefully secured.

"Let's go!" the senior firearms officer ordered.

Alex's explosives man was already on his way, his oppo covering him on his way forward. Nothing moved, no signs of life. It might have been easier to cut through the aluminium sheet wall, but no-one was sure if there was brickwork behind it. Better safe than sorry, and the explosion would neutralise any welcome party should there be one, at least for a few seconds.

The charge was placed, the two men withdrawing to shelter, then BOOM, and the plastic explosive had done it's work, a hole appearing where the corrugated wall had once been.

Alex was first through the jagged gap, his number two close behind, the two men dropping to their knees, weapons sweeping arcs, looking for trouble. The other two SAS men moved swiftly past them, heading towards the source of the light, a small office. All around them were pallets, small boxes on most of them, some stacked on metal shelving.

"Somebody coming out of the office," came over the headsets.

A man appeared in the office doorway, a second following him, both looking disorientated, both armed with handguns. They saw the soldiers, saw that they were outnumbered, turned towards the front of the building as the doo collapsed inwards, the police moving swiftly through it.

"Police! Put down your weapons!" the lead man ordered.

The two Albanians looked at each other, one shaking his head. It was clea that they were beaten, that taking up the fight was simply to die.

Their pistols clattered to the concrete floor, their arms shooting skywards.

The battle was over, not a shot fired.

Andile got the kids in the car before nine o'clock, her intention to get to the hotel in Bristol by eleven. If they were lucky, their room would be ready, anc if not the manager had already agreed that they could make use of the poo facilities.

She took the A40 into Wales, following the signs for Newport. She was stil undecided on whether to follow the M48 down to Chepstow, or to take the slightly longer and probably quicker route down on the M4 to cross the Severn. Both had been good to her in the past, but both had a chance o' congestion along the way. In the end, she opted for the motorway and the main Severn Bridge. It's tolls had been cancelled since 2018 to appease the Welsh government, and the satnav indicated that it would save her twenty minutes journey time.

Young Alex sat in the passenger seat beside her, happy to be riding shotgun just like his father. Her daughter slept in the back seat, the day too young for her liking. 'Just like her mother' she mused.

As she approached the giant bridge she glanced into her rear-view mirror noting that a truck unit without a trailer had been about forty metres back from her since joining the M4. Something, or nothing? Being married to the colonel of Britain's elite had rubbed off on her, her suspicious mind noting far more than was normally necessary.

'Probably nothing,' she guessed. The roads were pretty empty, the Saturday 'getting to work' traffic gone.

Young Alex gazed down at the vast expanse of water way below him watching sailors making the best of their weekend break. The snoring from the back seat confirmed the baby of the family was still out of it.

The second of the massive bridge support structures was approaching fast, the crossing almost done. She glanced in the rear-view mirror again, a sixth sense drawing her eyes there.

The lorry unit was much closer now, crossing into the fast lane, trying to overtake, fast without the load of a trailer and container. She picked it up in her side mirror, watching as it moved alongside. Her sons eyes moved towards it, the engine noise attracting him.

"Mum!" he suddenly yelled, pointing.

Too late, she turned her head, watched as the juggernaut came within inches of her car, swerving hard into it. She tried to avoid the collision, knew that there was nowhere to go.

The driver swung his wheel over hard, smashing his vehicle into the smaller car, the driver trying to avoid him, having no room to do so. He saw sparks from between the two vehicles, heard the crash as they connected, kept edging the Volvo lorry over to his left, forcing it towards the railings, the weakest part of the bridge structure. More sparks as the car was sandwiched between the rails and the truck, and then the barrier surrendered, let the car run off the road, off the bridge.

He didn't slow down, kept pushing on, trying to spot where the car would land in the freezing waters of the Severn.

They were airborne, flying from the giant bridge, the waters below still a good fifty metres from the shoreline. Andile wondered how deep the water would be, whether they would be able to get out, to swim to shore.

Then the car impacted with the solid surface of the water, the windscreen shattering, water flooding in immediately, the car ploughing a path into the depths.

Her last thoughts were that her suspicious mind had been correct.

And that she knew she would never see her husband and her children ever again.

The roadside services were less than a kilometre from the point of impact, the driver feeling a slight shake in his steering, knowing that he likely had a puncture. He kept going, headed for a lonely corner of the parking area, a place already agreed on.

He stopped, opened the door, got out, taking plastic gloves from this hands. It wouldn't really matter – the truck was rigged to burn, his DNA was never going to be found, but belt and braces was the name of the game. He knew that the bridge had cameras, but a peaked cap would have made him almost unidentifiable. He took the lid from a plastic container, tipped the petrol from it into the truck cabin, something to start the blaze.

He looked around, watched as a black BMW cruised over, his ride out of there.

Lighting the rag in his hand, he tossed it into the fuel soaked cabin.

His job was done.

Back in central London, they were halfway through the debrief when Alex was called outside. The raid had been a total success; no deaths, no injuries, a tonne of cannabis and other assorted drugs impounded. For once the police were on to a winner, their men and women heroes and not zeroes.

"What's wrong?" he asked once clear of the meeting room. He didn't fail to notice that it was Janet Anderson who was there to meet him. The head of MI6 didn't leave her desk just to meet up with anybody. Something was wrong.

Janet blushed, struggling to find the right words to say. In the end, she just gave up, said it as it was. "Andile is dead," she told her friend. "And both of the children. I'm so sorry."

Alone

Alex's first reaction to the news was disbelief.

It was simply impossible. He'd spoken to his wife just the day before, encouraged her to take the children for a weekend break, to buy their school uniforms for the new term, to have a family weekend without him. The world was good, his tight family circle happy.

And now they were dead.

"How did it happen?" he finally asked, the SAS soldier again kicking in.

"We're still piecing it together," Janet replied, finding it hard to maintain eye contact with the now angry man in front of her. "The car came off the Severn Bridge, landed in the river. We're still trying to recover it." She swallowed, knowing that her next words would be hard to accept. "From the bridge CCTV, it looks as if they were rammed off the road. A large lorry." There was little doubt that the 'accident' had been a planned attack, and she knew that Alex would swiftly put the parts together. He had led a successful attack against the mafia, and just a short time later his family had been killed. There were almost no dots to join.

"I want to see the footage."

Janet nodded, an expected request. "Let's grab a cuppa and I can show you on my laptop," she offered, indicating a nearby office.

Alex followed her, his temperament icy. Someone had just murdered his family, and that someone was now his personal target.

A couple of minutes later, sat beside the head of MI6, he watched as the family car was smashed from the road, the bridge railing first withstanding the collision, but then giving way after a second sideways shunt. The recording held the car for a second, then the vehicle disappeared from the camera's vision, heading down towards the waters below.

"I need names, Janet," the soldier ordered, his voice coldly calm.

Janet knew that he needed much more than that. He needed time out, a chance to reflect on what had just happened, possibly why. Alex was too involved, too close to the problem. He would need to be taken away from his job, moved aside until his judgement was normal again, unimpaired by his personal loss.

"We're working on that too," the head of MI6 replied. It was true, and it was what the soldier needed to hear right now. The reality of the situation would wait until later.

"I need to see where it happened."

It was something that Janet had expected, been fully prepared for. "My car is waiting," she said. "We have also found the burnt out lorry in a motorway services. Let's go. I'll show you everything."

The man needed the truth, but only in stages. First off, she needed to bring her friend back to planet earth, to stop him going rogue.

"Come on," she said softly.

The raid had cost Shehu over a hundred million in sales at street value, an awful but not irreplaceable hole in his finances. His mark-ups were immense, and a few future deliveries would soon fix the problem.

His bigger problem was restructuring his drug operation, finding a new and safe outlet, a place to run the business from. That would take longer, and a temporary fix would be needed in the short-term, something close to home and well defended. It would also need to be something decentralised, harder to hit with the better organised police assaults on his organisation. And that would make it harder to control.

Shehu's main concern was the call that was bound to come soon from Tirana. The loss of Sula was now added to by the loss of the drugs operation. How would the senior families at home react to that? What would they decide to do with him?

Taking out a part of the cause for recent events would work in his favour, but would it be enough to retain his role as the UK Krye? Was killing a family enough to keep his position?

He sat in his office trying to think of ways to re-establish control of the marketplace. Taking down the leader of the SAS was high on his agenda, something to reaffirm his power. Killing the monster that was hurting his people here in the UK.

It was the perfect place to start.

The trip to the crash site was a blur, Janet doing most of the talking, mainly talking about her work, her relationship with Mike Sanders, anything except the here and now. Alex understood what she was doing, had seen the horror on the faces of partners of men he'd lost in action. Breaking the news to them had been a task he'd made his own, a job that broke his heart each and every time. None of this helped him. Nothing could have prepared him for this moment. Nothing.

The bridge was already back in action, traffic moving in both directions, not busy but not bare. He'd almost expected it to be fenced off, the scene of a crime.

"Do you want to go to the area where the accident happened?" Janet asked him. "It's been temporarily blocked with safety barriers, so not much to see," she added, hoping to dissuade him.

"Please," he answered vacantly. In his mind it was important, it made everything real.

They walked along a maintenance lane, police tape stopping the ghouls and media from getting any closer. The railings were gone over a thirty metre section, part of them flapping in the high wind coming off the water, bent and twisted out over the Severn. A galvanised grey temporary fence blocked the gap.

Janet went as close as they were permitted, stood and waited while Alex stared at the mess. It was cold out there, and she hoped that he would soon want to move off, but it was as if he was in a trance.

"I can show you the burnt out lorry if you like," she offered, trying to move things along.

Alex stood another two minutes gazing at the waves below, looked then at the road, noted the scarring on its surface, no doubt the scene of the initial collision.

'I don't need to see it," he finally answered. "The police can handle that part. I just need names."

Janet nodded agreement once more. This wasn't the time to debate whether Alex was in any condition to continue his duties. It was time to take him home. Mike was waiting in Hereford. As an ex-SAS man himself, he'd know better the words to say.

"You need to take a step back for a while," Mike Sanders said, the three of them now in Alex's home. "And I'd like you to move into the officers mess," he added. "It's more secure until we are sure who is behind all of this."

"The Albanians," Alex replied softly, noting that his home was just as he'd left it, one of young Alex's video games in its box by the telly, Andile's work shoes in the hallway, his daughters tiny shoes next to them. "It all fits. I hit them twice, and then this happens. It's them."

"That's the most likely suspects," Mike agreed. "But you have made a few enemies over the years, so we need to play it safe." He was sure that Alex was correct, as was Janet, but right now he needed to put him somewhere safe. There were few safer places than Stirling Lines, surrounded by people who had the utmost respect for their leader, who would make certain that his life was not placed in any further danger. Plan B would be having those same people covertly guarding Alex's home – but that was something that the SAS officer would quickly identify and rally against.

Alex hmphed at Mike's words, unable to stop himself. "It's the Albanian mafia, no two ways about it," he said. "But I agree to stay in camp for now. Living here will be too much," he added, gesturing around the room.

Mike sighed, a small victory won. Pulling the wool over Alex's eyes was never going to happen, he was more than certain of that. He had mentored the man, brought him up through the ranks, supported his appointment. They'd been colleagues and friends through all sorts of hell. "Thank you for that," he said. "Do you need to pack a bag?"

Alex grimaced. "I'll be a minute," he replied, getting up and heading for the stairs. If there was one thing that he was absolutely dreading, it was this; going back into his bedroom, the place that Andile and himself had shared so many intimate moments, created their own small world. Two kids.

And now it was all gone, and he knew who to blame.

Now he just needed to know where to find the people behind it. Then to eradicate them from the face of the earth.

The Albanian watched the three people leave the house, noted that others left soon afterwards, people that he had not even noticed until that point. It reminded him of where he was – the home of Britain's elite military force, the Special Air Service.

He phoned Shehu, his report short and to the point.

"I think it would be suicide, boss," he said at the end. "This is his turf, and his people. Some of the best soldiers anywhere."

The mafia leader considered the statement, nodded silently to himself. "Get yourself back up to London," he finally ordered. "I need to think this through." Carefully, he added to himself.

Mike stayed on in the mess with Alex, a place of so many great memories for him, but now a place full of sadness. Everyone in the Regiment was aware of what had happened, knew that their leader was hurting. They'd all lost colleagues over the years – it came with the job – but losing family was something else, especially when that loss involved young children. There was a tension in the air, no-one knowing what to say to help.

How do you help a man who has just lost everything? Even Alex's closest friends didn't have a satisfactory answer to that one.

"Are you coming for a bite to eat?" Mike asked as the evening meal drew closer. "Maybe a pint at the bar?"

The soldier shook his head, knowing that food was essential, knowing also that he couldn't face it yet. "I'll give it a miss," he said. "Maybe later." He sat alone in his room, the television news running.

Mike nodded, his own appetite almost non-existent. Too much pain. He'd been a friend of Andile, had known the children well, almost like an uncle to the two of them. "No problem."

But he knew that it was a problem. Alex was bottling everything up, ready to explode.

"I'll knock on your door later. We can grab a toastie at the bar. Something light." He had to try and engage his friend, get him talking.

Alex nodded, turned back to the TV.

With Mike gone, Alex phoned Janet Anderson, now on her way back to the capital.

"Any names yet? Any leads?" he asked, straight to the point.

"Nothing yet Alex," she responded. And even if she had something, she knew that handing that intel over to the SAS colonel right now was not a great idea. "Is Mike there with you?" she asked, trying to move away from the subject.

"He's gone for food."

"You should join him," Janet countered. She understood that eating was probably the last thing on the soldier's mind, but also knew that he needed to look after himself. "A bit of food, a beer or two, an early night," she added.

A silence followed, getting uncomfortable. "You're not going to give me the names even if you have them, are you?"

Janet glanced down at the speedo, noticed that she was doing seventy-five, forced herself to focus on driving safely. "It's not like that," she said, her voice tense. "We have suspects, but we need confirmation before we go in all guns blazing."

Alex said nothing, feeling that he was being frozen out. "Okay," he allowed. It was the best he could do for now. He wanted to avenge the murder of his family, knew that the authorities probably wouldn't allow him to do that. It was too personal. He would be seen as unstable, a risk to others around him. Shoot first, ask later.

And he knew that they were probably right.

"We need to step back," the man in Tirana said, not only the head of a mafia clan over there, but also a very senior politician in the city. "We are going head-to-head with the British Army here, and not just any old unit of their military." He paused, looked across the table at his brother, another senior member of the Albanian authorities. "It will be too costly, a massive disruption to our operations over there."

Luan Shehu could read the hints, could see where the conversation was leading. "So what do you want me to do?" he asked anyway.

"Come home," the voice commanded. It wasn't a request, it was an order.

"Who will look after the business over here?" Shehu asked. Going home was not what he wanted. There he was just another gang member. Here in the UK he was the leader. The Krye.

"I will organise that."

Shehu sighed, nodded to himself. There was no choice here. If he crossed these people, then he'd be signing his own death warrant. "I'll organise flights, send your people the details," he said.

"Good man, Shehu. It is a temporary measure, a cooling down period. We will meet when you are here, plan for the future."

Plan for the future? Luan Shehu said nothing, but in his mind he could only think of one future. Killing the SAS colonel who had ruined his present and recent past. That was the only future that mattered.

"I will see you soon."

"We need to take him off the case," Ruth instructed the Zoom meeting of herself and three others. Janet Anderson, Mary Kemp, and Mike Sanders had joined the meeting from their various UK locations, Mike the only one physically close to the man they were all discussing.

"He's not really 'on the case' as such," Kemp reminded them all. "He's a soldier, not a policeman. He was just there for support."

"That's splitting hairs," Ruth countered, not in the mood for such trivia. "We all know exactly what I mean. He's hurting, his family are dead, and we cannot afford to allow him to continue fighting the Albanians." In those few words she'd just verbalised everything that the others felt. Alex was in danger of becoming a loose cannon.

"But how do we present that to him?" Janet asked, a frown on her face. "How do you tell a soldier that he can't track down the criminals that have just destroyed his whole life?"

That was the million dollar question. A silence followed it, no-one happy to be the one to relay the message.

Mike put his head in his hands, closed his eyes. Of all of them, he was the soldier, the one who had served with Alex, who understood the dangers of battle, the closeness of death. It didn't help him to understand exactly what his comrade was going through right now, but it put him closer to it than the others.

He raised his head, looked into his laptop camera. "Has anyone spoken to Andile's family yet?" he asked. "I'm thinking Nkosi, and her sister Kaya. Have they been informed?"

He could tell by the blank looks on the faces in their individual screens that the answer was no.

"Okay," he cut in. "Let me talk to Nkosi. Let him do the dirty work."

Nkosi Sithole was an ex-British SAS soldier but was now a part of the South African SAS that had been pieced together by Alex Green to help restore order in the country post COVID. He was also Alex's brother-in-law, his wife Kaya the sister of Andile.

"Oh shit," were his first words when Mike broke the news. "No."

Mike waited a second, letting the facts sink in. "I'm afraid so mate," he finally allowed. "I'm really sorry to be the one bearing such bad news, but..." He let himself tail off. He'd been the colonel when Nkosi had been with 22 SAS, a unit small enough that everyone knew one another.

"I understand boss," the Zulu man answered. "Better from you than from some faceless official. You knew her, know Kaya, know me." He stopped, the realization suddenly hitting him that he would need to break the news to his wife.

The ex-colonel waited, weighing up his words carefully. "We believe that the killers were the Albanian mafia. Alex was being used to neutralise them, and we feel that they took his family as a soft target. You can imagine how he feels, what he'd like to do." He paused. "I don't think letting him loose right now would be a safe idea, not for himself, nor for the bad guys."

Nkosi sucked in a lungful of air, momentarily driving his grief away. "What do you want me to do?"

The call from his brother-in-law surprised Alex, making him recognise that in the madness of the past days he had totally neglected his family. He felt ashamed, knowing his own anguish had swamped everything else. He had forgotten about the people that were most dear to him. To Andile.

"Who told you?" he asked softly.

"Mike called," Nkosi replied, not needing to add a surname. "How are you, bro?"

Alex was silent for a long while. "Not great, brother," he finally said.

They had made Alex an honorary Zulu years before, a member of the extended family that they were all a part of. He had been so important in the post-COVID rebuilding of South Africa, then helped stop the trade in rhino horn, saving the country's wildlife, gone on to marry a Zulu wife. It hurt Nkosi to hear him sound so low.

"Come home, bro. Come back to your family."

Alex nodded silently to himself, a few tears finally falling down his face, the first since the terrible news. He knew that this was the right thing to do. He needed to go home, to rebuild himself.

And then he could take his revenge.

Home Africa

It was almost two months since his return to Durban, and though the memories were as difficult as the day he'd been informed of Andile's death, the pain was slowly fading. He was certain that it would never completely go away, that his life would never be the same, but he was sleeping better at night, taking better care of himself. Having others around him that were sharing the same pain made it a little easier to bear.

He was down on the beach at Umhlanga Rocks, running on the sand, close to the breaking waves, working his body. He found that hard exercise stopped him thinking too much, focussed his mind on beating the miles. Initially Nkosi had joined him, forcing the pace, retraining his mind, but now he was happy to do it alone. It was a benefit to his body, but more than that, it was a release for his thoughts. From his SAS training, Alex knew that getting the brain right was far more important than conditioning the body. If the brain said 'yes' then the body would follow.

The first week had been the worst, sitting with his family, talking to the children. Andile had been the last living person in Kaya's family, her parents taken by the COVID virus. Losing her sister had smashed the life out of her. It had meant that Alex had to forget his own problems, to help Nkosi nurse his sister-in-law through the agony.

He'd worked with it and found that helping others had helped him to fix himself.

He was almost as far as Umdloti now, about three miles up from Umhlanga, four miles from his home. He allowed himself to slow to a stop, took off his T-shirt and running shoes, turned to the Indian Ocean. He could see a couple of dolphins in the sloping waves, animals that had no time for grief. He ran through the waves, knowing that he'd never get close to them, but happy to be sharing the water with such fabulous creatures.

He swam out about fifty metres, full speed front crawl, stopped, treading water, looking for the dolphins. After a minute, he gave up, swam slowly back towards the beach.

The sun was warm on his skin, quickly drying him. Shrugging on his top, he wiped the sand from his feet, pulled on his trainers. He stared at the ocean.

The dolphins were still out there, just invisible now. It meant he had no more excuses to rest. They'd soon be gone and so would he.

He set off at a sprint, pushing the pace, making his only focus the pain in his body as he ran as fast as he possibly could.

"I've been given a name," Janet Anderson told Mary Kemp, spymaster to spymaster. "It's come from one of our contacts in Italy, a covert source in Puglia, so we need to be careful with the intel. The man's trying to infiltrate the Sacra Corona Unita, so I'm sure you understand what I mean."

Kemp sipped her coffee, nodded. "They say they have links with the Albanians," she said softly. "Combined smuggling ops, drugs, others."

"It's true," the MI6 chief confirmed. "Maybe more, but we're working on it."

"And they have a name for the man here in England?"

Janet shook her head. "No, not really," she allowed. "They have a name for the man who was the head honcho here. It seems he was recalled, that now he's working things down there. He's actually the Albanian link man to Sacra Corona."

Mary Kemp sighed. "So no further forward for me then?"

A shrug from Janet. "Something to follow up on," she said. "His name might lead you to others."

The MI5 director nodded. "True," she agreed. "You'll send me the details?"

"Today."

"Will you pass those details on to our SAS friend?"

Janet frowned, unsure whether she should even answer the question. Both men under discussion were now out of the country, no longer a concern for the country's Security Service. "I'm not sure," she finally offered. "I'm not sure how he could assist us, or even if he's ready to get involved in this kind of thing yet. He went through a lot."

"I agree. Perhaps keep me in the loop. I know we've improved lots on information sharing, but it's easy to fall back into old practices..." Kemp let the message hang open. "I don't need everything, just a heads-up."

Janet nodded agreement. She would help where she could, but some secrets were best kept that way. And right now, she wasn't even sure herself of how to use this latest intel.

"You'll get it," was all she agreed.

Being the founder of the country's elite regiment, and having himself completed their training program voluntarily, Alex was afforded opportunities that others weren't. One of them was access to the South African SAS barracks and the use of their facilities, including the shooting ranges. He was there again today, keeping his skills alive.

The pistol range was indoors, shielded from the burning sun, it's targets able to be set-up at anything from ten to thirty metres. Firing a handgun at a target at a greater range was like getting a hole-in-one on the golf course – more luck than judgement.

His magazine empty, he cleared the weapon and set it down to one side, pressed a button to draw in his targets. He'd been working at thirty metres, fired off the whole thirteen rounds of his Sig Sauer P226, a weapon he was fully familiar with from Hereford, and also the favoured handgun of the South African troops. He studied the target, happy that all of his shots had passed close to centre, the spread only about three-and-a-half inches.

"You've still got it then?" a voice said from behind him. He turned to see Nkosi watching.

"It's not too bad," he allowed. "Are you having a go?"

"Why not?" the Zulu said, accepting the challenge. "It's been a while since we had a contest."

Alex showed that the pistol was safe, handed it over to his brother-in-law. "All yours," he said, passing on a box of ammunition. "Loser pays the beers tonight." He grinned at Nkosi, the gauntlet tossed down.

"Do we tell Alex?" Janet asked Mike, the two of them back in their shared flat close to Twickenham.

Mike quickly considered the question, weighing up the possible outcomes.

"I guess the real question is, what is your long term plan? Do you intend taking this guy Shehu down, or do you just clock him, let the Italians take him in. And if you want the man, then how do you do it? Alex is a soldier. Can you run a military operation down in Italy or Albania?"

Janet sipped her glass of red wine, pleased to be bouncing her thoughts off someone who would keep them to himself.

"You're right," she conceded. "We couldn't run a mission down there, at least not overtly. It should be the locals doing the work."

"But..."

Mike could read her like a book, knew that there was more to be said than she was showing on the surface. "But he was the man running what was basically a terror operation here in the UK. He was targeting our police force, men that normally carry no firearms." She halted herself, aware that she was getting angry. "I want him gone," she finally admitted.

"Can't your people do that?" the ex-soldier asked.

A slow nod came in answer. "But it would be a lot of red tape to cut through, and if it went wrong it would screw up our relations with Italy, maybe with the European Union intelligence community as a whole. It would be risky. A deniable operation against both the Albanian Mafia and the Sacra Corona, carried out on their home turf." She shrugged. "Without any real sort of back-up."

"Put like that, I can see the problems," Mike said with a smile. He poured two more glasses of wine. "Let me sleep on it. Maybe a great idea will pop up."

"Back to the original question. Do I tell Alex? He's on the other side of the world, he's been out of action for about two months, and he's alone. What can he do to help?"

Mike stared into space for a second, trying to put himself in Alex Green's place. "It's a tough one," he said. "Let's put it this way – if we don't tell him, how will that influence our future work with him? Will he forgive us? Will that be the end of him and us?"

"And what would Ruth say if we destroyed her relationship with her favourite soldier?" Janet grinned. "Our favourite soldier," she corrected.

"And what if we do tell him and he goes off on a lone wolf mission?" Mike asked, realizing that this was also a strong possibility. "The man ordered the execution of his family. That is certainly enough to tip most people over the top."

Janet nodded. This wasn't a simple equation, and balancing things would be tough. Saying something might just trigger a private war. Not being open and honest would possibly lose a serious asset for the UK, not to mention a good friend.

"Let's do as you suggested and sleep on it. Hopefully we'll both wake up with an answer we can agree on."

They clinked glasses, the discussion closed for the evening.

It was the call that Alex had been waiting for, praying that somehow it would actually happen. It was also something that he'd keep hidden from his family, a secret treasure that he'd save for himself.

"Luan Shehu," he muttered to himself, the call with Janet now done.

He had a name, and more importantly, he had a rough location. Now he could begin planning. Taking on the mafia on their home ground would not be simple. Taking them on without the back-up of his own soldiers would be even tougher. But he didn't want to fight the mafia.

He had a name, the man who had caused his family's demise. He wanted to fight Luan Shehu.

"It's done," the MI6 chief told her partner.

Mike Sanders remained silent for a beat, again trying to put himself in Alex's mind. "I'll let Nkosi know the name in a day or two, see if Alex has shared or not," he replied.

"And then we'll know more," Janet said. "Do we have a lone wolf, or is he ready to return, to fight with the team."

She knew that what she was doing was pure manipulation, playing with a man's life. She also knew that it was her job to put her country ahead of friendship and feelings, and her country needed to send a signal to the crime gangs that were overrunning it. Taking down Luan Shehu would be a perfect signal. Especially on his home turf.

"I just hope that it's the latter," Mike said, interrupting her thoughts.

Janet didn't answer. Perhaps the lone wolf was the better solution for England. Getting approval to do it any other way was not going to be easy at all.

Moving On

Planning and preparation was everything. Even in his early basic military training, Alex had been taught the five Ps – Planning Prevents Piss Poor Performance. As an elite soldier, this had only been reinforced. Planning was everything, and preparing for every eventuality you could envisage was a massive part of it. From experience, Alex also knew that however amazing the plan was, it could always go awry. Being ready for that – and having a Plan B and C – helped you win through.

When he'd first arrived back in Durban he had quietly started his rebuild. The physical aspects he couldn't hide, and his military skills also needed tools – weapons, explosives, vehicles – that he couldn't get his hands on easily. They were the overt preparation.

Behind the scenes, he'd started studying Albania and the corrupt culture of the place. It was a poor country, and many of the problems stemmed from this. But he needed to know more, to understand the mindset of the people, especially those who made up the mafia segment of the population.

And now he had a new topic to study. Puglia, Italy.

Knowing your enemy was critical in taking them down. What were their strengths and weaknesses? Who were their main players, and where were they centred? How did they operate?

In his one room apartment he studied everything he could find about the two countries. Slowly he built up a picture, and with it a plan began to take form.

Luan Shehu reflected for possibly the hundredth time in the last two months on why he'd been so pissed off at the thought of leaving England. Okay, his homeland was poor, but that was all relative; in his senior position, he lived like a king, even if those around him generally had nothing except the scraps from his table. And the weather... well, here he was on a forty foot long speedboat, leaving the Port of Vlora, the temperature just over thirty Celsius, the sea flat calm. It was almost like being a tourist, but with a better boat.

The skipper manoeuvred the vessel around fishing boats and leisure craft, the old port cranes temporarily throwing the boat into their shadows. Shehu glanced back at the two girls they were transporting over to Brindisi in Italy, one sixteen, the other fifteen, briefly wondering about their future, but deciding that they'd never had one anyway. They came from the countryside, thought that they were on their way to the big city, a chance to make some real money, have a life. In truth they were being sold to Sacra Corona Unita, the SCU, an Italian mafia organisation that his own people collaborated with in drugs and people smuggling deals. These two would become the toys of one of the SCU's kingpins for a short while, then be traded on the streets. They'd be lucky to last a year.

Right now they sat in their bikinis on the wide sofa seat at the back of the vessel, sunning themselves like a couple of celebrities. Why ruin their fun? Shehu thought. That would come soon enough.

His other cargo for the journey was far less visible. Below deck, five hundred kilos of Afghan crystal meth would soon be making the sea crossing to Puglia. The Albanian mafia had been the conduit for the Afghan drug trade to southern Italy for years now, working hand-in-hand with the Sacra Corona to supply the streets.

In the end, Shehu reflected, the job here in his homeland was not so much different to what he'd been doing back in London. It was easier, all of the trade already established, the connections made. The police on both sides of the water generally turned a blind eye, unlike the authorities back in the UK. Backhanders went a lot further down here.

And yes, he thought, leaning back in his on-deck captain's chair, and smiling – the weather was a thousand times more acceptable.

Carlo 'Il Porco' Messi had risen to the dizzy heights of the Società Segreta, the top level leadership of the Sacra Corona Unita, just over three years previously, putting him in a position of almost absolute power. He'd been 'baptized' into the SCU at the tender age of sixteen, had become ranked as a 'Lo Sgarro' only three years later, a rank only obtained on having killed at least three enemies in the course of his 'duties'. It allowed him to form his own team, his own 'filiale'.

His title 'The Pig' had been gained along the way. Carlo had belonged to the farming community as a boy, had always lived in wonder that pigs would eat anything that you fed them. This extended to his victims. Pigs left no evidence.

He leaned his elbows on his balcony rail, looked out over the sparkling sea. The SCU had turned over a cool eight hundred million euros in drug trading in the last twelve months, just short of that in prostitution. The same again if you combined the incomes of weapon deals and extortion. Not too bad for a country boy.

And more was on its way right now. He didn't like the Albanians, but he had to take his hat off to their work ethic. He asked for whatever goods he wanted, they supplied them.

Another bonus to being the boss was that if he wanted, he then got to trial the goods. And with this new delivery he'd already seen the computer images of the two teenagers that would soon be earning him another income stream. Eventually.

Tonight he was in for a treat.

Gianluigi Maldini watched as the speedboat approached the quayside, the engine now down to idle. He had become a manovalanza – a worker – having now completed his forty day trial period as a picciotti, or apprentice. He'd sworn his devotion and his life to the SCU just days before, proving that he wasn't an impostor from the authorities, and now he was being trusted for the first time with real business.

He moved to the quay edge as the vessel's captain threw out a line, caught it and swiftly pulled it around a bollard, helping to stop the boat as it glided alongside. Another manovalanza secured the stern line, quickly tying it off. The captain shut off the engine, made adjustments to his other controls, and closed the computer system down.

"Gian, you go down and see how many men they want," the senior worker instructed him. "With a bit of luck, just you," he quipped.

Gianluigi grinned, happy to be a part of the real operation, to earn his spurs. He climbed down a few steps of a quayside ladder, stepped across the gap and onto the deck. "Do you need anything from us?" he asked a man near the stern of the boat. "Anything to unload, arrange a refuel, whatever?" He noticed two young girls behind the man, both carrying small cases.

"I'll need a car," the man answered. His accent gave away the fact that he wasn't local, quite likely from across the water in Albania. "But you can also help me with moving some of the boxes," he added.

"Is there much to move?"

"About half a tonne," the man answered. Gianluigi was about to laugh but noticed that the man was deadly serious. Half a tonne of drugs. He could hardly imagine it.

"I'll get some help," he replied, careful to hide his surprise.

"I'd advise that too," the Albanian responded. "Otherwise you're going to be here all week." He laughed at his own joke, turned to the two girls behind him, both looking a little pensive now. "But first off, get me the car. I need to deliver a gift to your leader." He made a small nodding gesture towards the women.

"I'll be right back," the young Italian replied. He was new to all of this but guessed that this was what the others labelled 'fresh meat'. The thought suddenly made him feel a little sick, but he put on his best poker face and climbed back up the ladder.

Il Porco shook hands with Shehu, gave him a swift brotherly hug. He had no love for the man, but you should never bite the hand that feeds. He gave the two girls a quick once over, a head to foot inspection, slowing at his main points of interest. They looked as good 'in the flesh' as they had in the computer photos.

He turned to an older woman who hovered by the doorway. "Take the ladies to their rooms," he ordered. "They can unpack, use the pool, freshen up. They will both join me for dinner tonight."

The two ladies glanced at one another, a small smile exchanged between themselves. A luxury boat ride, a villa that was like something from the television, a host who was treating them to dinner. Life was great.

The older lady took them away, leaving the men to themselves.

"And the ice?" Il Porco asked, the street name for the meth.

"Five hundred kilos. As you ordered."

The Pig nodded, running the sums through his head, working out profit margins. The results were all satisfactory. "Thank you," he replied. "Are you staying with us for dinner this evening?" he asked.

Shehu had not expected this, had come unprepared for a night away, but knew that a negative reply would probably offend. "If you have the space, then of course," he said. He would make excuses to escape for an hour or two, buy some spare clothing in town. "I'd be honoured."

"Good," the Pig nodded. "Let's say seven-thirty for dinner. I'll get Martha to show you to your quarters."

The Italian turned away, exiting at the far end of the room. He also had things to do. Money wasn't made by sitting on your arse, and he now had a shedload of meth to get on to the streets. He needed his team to cut up the consignment, bulk it up with additives, and get it out to the sellers. His network would make short work of it all, and he would add to his fortune.

Not a bad day at the office.

The girls weren't laughing now, not one bit of a smile showing on their battered faces or shattered bodies. They were broken, just pieces of meat ready to be passed on to others, to be abused and sold on, just tools for the making of money. They would be transported in the morning, their documents taken from them, tying them to the pimps that would sell their bodies to anyone with the right money.

Shehu and Il Porco sat together on the balcony, a bottle of cognac on the table beside them, cigars in hand, content.

"That was excellent," the Italian said after a minute's silence, exhaling a lungful of aromatic smoke towards the moon.

"The food or the women?" the Albanian asked with a wry smile, hoping not to offend his host.

"The food of course," The Pig answered, enjoying the joke. "The girls were just entertainment," he added.

"Then I was very well entertained," Shehu replied. He picked up his glass, saluted his host. "To great food and lively entertainment," he toasted, his smile wide.

Il Porco returned the toast. "To a better night next time," he said, downing half of his brandy.

"Better and better," Shehu saluted in return, his misgivings about leaving London long gone. Life was looking up.

Time To Go Visit

"Have you heard from Alex recently?" Janet asked Mike, the two sharing breakfast in their Twickenham flat. It was a Sunday ritual that they always tried hard to honour, though with Janet's position, it was often spoiled.

"I've left him alone for a while," the ex-SAS colonel replied. "If he chose not to tell Nkosi about the target, it means that he's either trying to go it alone, or that he wants to draw a line under all of that, to just become a civilian again."

Janet shook her head. "I see no chance of that," she said. "I was the one to break the news to him. He was withdrawn, but you could see the anger. He'll not let things rest, of that I'm sure."

"Maybe I should have another chat with Nkosi?"

"Probably a good idea. Just to find out how he's filling his time. If he's preparing for something then it will probably be pretty obvious, especially to his family."

Mike glanced at his watch, gave a small shake of his head. "Tomorrow," he said. "It's their Sunday over there too. Let them have a bit of peace."

Janet took a bite of toast, expression thoughtful. "Maybe I should find an excuse for a trip down there. See things with my own eyes." Things had calmed in London with Luan Shehu off the scene, the attacks on the police service halted. It was clear that the man must have had something to do with the targeting, that the Albanians had been ordered to back off.

Alex wanted revenge, but so did Janet. And she knew that he was the right weapon to get it.

"So, how's he doing?" Mike asked the following day.

"He seems better, more concerned with his own wellbeing now. When he first got back it was hard to get him out, but now he's back into running. We even had a shooting contest the other day, a few beers afterwards." Nkosi paused, wondering what else to add. "What happened to him will never be fully healed," he continued. "But I think there might be some light at the end of the tunnel."

"Does he mention Albania at all?"

"Not really. He told me about the police killings, why he was involved in the operation against the mafia crowd. He blames himself for that leading to Andile's targeting, realises that her and the family should have been given more protection." Nkosi sighed. "Hindsight's a great thing. He'll always think it was his fault."

"I'm sorry, mate," Mike replied. "It's good that he has you and the family to fall back on. He needs it."

"Yeah, I know," the Zulu replied. "But even that's hard. Every time that Kaya sees him, it reminds her that she'll never see her sis again. Tough love."

Mike hesitated for a moment, then decided to open up a little more. "Janet's considering a trip down there. Some official stuff for Six, but she could swing by and spend a few days in Durbs. Would that help?"

"A change is as good as a rest, they say. It would be a distraction."

"I'll keep you in the picture."

"Should I tell Alex?"

Mike considered the question, trying to decide if his partner would prefer to keep it quiet, deciding that it would be out in the open as soon as she got there anyway. "Why not?" he replied. "As you said, it's a nice distraction for him. Give him something to look forward to."

A foreign language was something that Alex could certainly not include on his CV. He had a smattering of languages from the countries he'd operated in, enough to get the gist of what was going on, but by no means was he a linguist. As far as both Albanian and Italian went, he basically had the sum total vocabulary of zilch.

He'd visited Italy, never Albania. His experience was limited to tourist trips; Milan, Rome, Venice, Pisa, all city breaks with Andile. He'd never been to the south of the country, never anywhere past Rome.

There was no way that he could pass himself off as a local in either country, that was for certain. To learn either language would take months, years if he wanted to be fluent. He simply didn't have time for that. He was going to have to be a tourist. A tourist who had far too much interest in criminal activities. He'd stand out like a sore thumb.

His phone buzzed and he closed his laptop cover, reading the name on the cell. Nkosi.

"Hey, bro, what's up?" he asked, expecting an invite to dinner, possibly a beer somewhere. His brother-in-law had been a great support, but he hadn't even confided his plans to him, convinced that he would either try to talk him out of it, or insist on joining him on a suicide mission.

"Just had a call from Mike," the Zulu replied. "It seems that Janet is thinking of a visit down here soon. Something official, but also a trip across to see us."

Alex's radar antennae went on to full alert, sensing that there might be more to this message than initially met the eye. Yes, Janet was an old friend, one who'd been involved in several hotspots with him over the years, a lady who'd seen her own share of action. She'd also been the bearer of bad news following Andile's death, the one who had given him the name of Albanian mafia chief soon afterwards. Why was she coming to South Africa, and more importantly, why was she coming to meet with him? Friendship?

Alex didn't think so. Janet did little without having a strong motive.

"Something to look forward to," he finally offered, sensing that Nkosi was waiting for a response. "Did he give a date?"

"No, just that she was looking into a visit. Something to do with the Firm, work related stuff."

"Maybe I should give her a call," Alex suggested. "Make a plan."

"Why ever not."

"Why do you want to go to South Africa?" Ruth Maybank asked her friend, certain that she wouldn't be getting a totally truthful answer.

"It's been a while," Janet said dismissively, flicking her fingers as if shooing off a bothersome fly. "And I thought that I could combine it with a visit to

Alex, see how he's recuperating. We could do with getting him back to Hereford, back into the driving seat."

The PM had to agree with that. They'd had a major holding Alex's position for the last few months, unwilling to replace the SAS colonel so soon after his loss. It was working okay but it wasn't a situation that could last forever. A stand-in could do so much, but couldn't implement real changes, or make his own mark on things. Either Alex needed to return to the fold, or someone else needed to be awarded the position.

"That's fair enough," Ruth conceded, still troubled that she might be missing something. The two had known one another since university, but she was well aware that the spy chief often had her own agenda, things that she didn't feel the PM needed to be burdened with. "Please keep me in the picture," she added. Hopefully that would be enough to ensure she was informed of anything else that developed.

Or maybe not.

"Is this anything to do with the Albanian shit?" Alex asked the head of MI6. "I'm guessing that it's not just a jolly, or just to see your favourite SAS man," he added, forcing his tone to be a little more friendly.

"It's a bit of both," Janet replied, noting the change. "But please keep that off the record. I need to get down there and touch base with my people up in Pretoria, but I also wouldn't mind a little time with you. Just to see how you are, what your future plans are. The world still needs good people."

Alex knew better than to ask too many questions over a personal cell phone, knew that someone, somewhere, would be monitoring his conversation, if not Janet's. "And when might I have the honour?" he asked.

"Not fixed yet," the lady replied. Or not willing to share yet, Alex surmised. "I'll get back to you in the next days. Within a week, that's for certain."

It was all a bit vague, but the SAS man knew that it was as much as he was likely to get. Covert operations were just that – covert. Janet had something to say but wanted to do it face to face. And if this was anything to do with what had happened to his family, he was pretty certain that things would be done well under the radar.

'Be good to see you," he eventually replied.

Janet nodded silently to herself, certain that Alex had understood her message.

It was time to go to Africa again.

Living On A Knife Edge

Basri Kola had been in the crime business basically since his birth, visiting unlucky extortion victims with his father from about the age of three, seeing grown men begging for another chance to pay off their debts before he even knew what a debt was. He went through school a bully, began being paid by the mafia at twelve for delivering messages, and took part in his first punishment beating at sixteen. By eighteen he was a fully-fledged 'Mik', responsible for organising the team to suit whatever activities that his current Boss had decided on.

It wasn't long before he graduated from that role, taking his own small clan of extended family members, making his own team, sometimes known as a 'fis'. But that wasn't enough for a still young Basri: his goal was to be at the top, and at fifty-two years of age, he was now there. Within the Vlora region there was no more senior mafia member.

Luan Shehu knew of the man's route to power, had heard of his exploits along the way. If all of the tales were true, the man had a terribly brutal past, had taken down not only the 'enemy', but also anyone who'd dared to stand in the way of his progress. He was a man to stay on the right side of. Not a man to cross.

"So you're enjoying your return to the homeland?" Basri was asking. "Away from that fucking freezing place over there."

Luan smiled gracefully, partly to humour the man, partly because Basri was right. "It's good to be home," he admitted, nodding. "The work is fun, but like you just said, the weather is a million times better."

"And the English are just too full of themselves. Been there, done it all, bloody condescending farts," the most feared man in Vlora said. "I was there once, hated the place. Their press are dreadful, their politicians full of bluster, no-one in control. 'Freedom of speech' they call it. If someone called me out in the newspapers, I'd have him bloody well castrated."

Shehu guessed that that was true. One hundred percent true if rumours were to be believed.

"And the Royal Family," the older man went on. "What a lot of bullshit! There's that one that's gone off to America, married some bloody bitch across there." He sipped a black coffee, nowadays his poison before five o'clock, a doctor's warning slowing his drinking days. "What sort of ass boasts about shooting Taliban members? The guy was sat in an Apache helicopter, probably a kilometre from the action, shooting at targets with a minigun. That's not fighting! And he says it was only twenty-five militants." He paused, puffing up his chest. "I'd killed more men than that before I reached twenty. All of them with a handgun, a knife, looking them in the eyes before they went, smelling their fear." He smiled, his eyes drifting away, recalling those days. "Different times."

Shehu nodded, a forced grin on his lips. "How can I help you today?" he asked. "I guess you didn't just invite me to talk about the old times?"

"You're right," the mafia leader agreed. He picked up a sheet of paper, tapped it with his index finger. "I've been looking at the work you've been doing with the Italians. You seem to be pulling good prices from that nutter across there in Puglia. The Pig."

"Thanks. Just doing what is expected," Shehu said humbly. "The forecasts look good for more of the same."

"Be careful with that Messi," Kola said quickly, halting the platitudes. "He is a double dealing bastard. He'll be your friend one day, your worst enemy the next. If he asks for credit, tell him where to go."

Shehu thought about his last visit to Brindisi, the excellent meal, the 'entertainment'. He carefully considered his next words. "So far he has been nothing but business-like," he finally said. "And all of his payments have been standard, half up-front."

"No invitations to banquets, no hookers?"

Lying was not a wise way forward, Luan Shehu knew that. To lie and to get caught out would end his career, possibly worse. "He surprised me last time with an invitation to dinner," he allowed, almost certain now that Kola must have spies across the water. The man had contacts everywhere, hadn't survived so long in this business by not keeping himself informed. "I'd also delivered two girls to him that day. He suggested trying them out." He glanced nervously at his boss.

"It's good that you told me," Kola replied swiftly. Something in Shehu's mind told him that the man had already known. "But keep your distance from him.

Business is business. Pleasure is pleasure. He will draw you in, ask for favours." He looked at his watch, made a decision. "We may work with him, but we do not belong to him." Another glance at his wrist. "And now that it is gone five o'clock, I think we need a drink."

Shehu shivered. Messi and Kola might be different nationalities, have different beliefs, but they were both very similar, driven, dangerous men. To cross either could be fatal.

Luan Shehu was being forced to walk a very precarious path, possible death lurking on both sides of it.

He would need to keep his wits about himself.

His next trip to Brindisi was little different from the previous one, three girls and a stack of drugs, this time a mix of meth and heroin from Afghanistan. The biggest change was a more personal one: how would he handle the advances of Il Porco? How could he keep two masters happy, and still benefit himself?

Since the meeting with Kola, Shehu had thought long and hard about the best way to move forward. He could do the sensible thing and stick with his own. He knew the ways of the Albanian Mafia, understood the rules, and what could happen if he broke them.

He guessed that the codes for the Sacra Corona were not much different. Cross them, and your life expectancy took a turn for the worse.

The question was, which one would reward him best?

And a second question was, could he play one against the other, receive reward from both, and get away with it? That was the get rich quick scheme, but the potential dangers it brought were terminal.

A third option was just to get out of the business, but that would only result in a life where he was always looking over his shoulder. Once in at his level, there was no way out. He simply knew too much.

He decided to take the path of least resistance, at least for the time being. Stay friends with both parties, play a canny hand, and hope for the best.

Il Porco checked over the new arrivals, quietly disappointed. They were older than the last girls, a little more street wise. The younger girls were usually more nervous, so afraid that they would do anything to please. These three would need breaking, softening up, or they'd be likely to try and do a runner, escape from their pimps. And that was bad for business.

He smiled at the Albanian, disguising his doubts. "So you'll be staying over this evening," he said, not a question. "We have the 'entertainment' right here, and I'm sure that the ladies would be pleased to join us for dinner." He smiled towards the women, got two doubtful looks in return, one nod.

"I was hoping to get back before dark," Shehu replied, actually the truth. He'd decided that this would be the safest option, especially if Kola had eyes in Brindisi.

"Come now..." The Pig said, pouting and pretending to be offended.

Shehu looked away, glanced towards the ladies. These were more to his taste than the last lot, girls with plenty of experience. More like the British girls he decided with half a grin.

"What's funny?" the Italian asked, a hint of anger in his tone.

The Albanian man swiftly straightened his face, held up his hands in a gesture of apology. "Nothing, nothing at all. I was just thinking how nice the ladies were looking, and how it would actually be rude to not accept your proposal. Of course I'll stay over."

Messi smiled, the sudden tension in the room dissipating with it. Even the girls seemed to relax a little. "Perfect," he said. "Let's say back here for dinner at seven. A night to remember for all of us," he continued, making a dramatic bow towards the women.

Two of them giggled, the third not so, obviously having a rough idea of what might be on the menu that evening. And it wasn't the food that bothered her.

Back on the boat to his homeland, Shehu reflected on the previous evening. It was as if his boss had written the script, that somehow he'd become a fortune teller.

Things had started much the same as before, great food, good Italian wines, the girls dressed by the housekeeper to attract a man. The streetwise lady had guessed what the end result was planned to be, had complained, so Messi had slapped her around a bit, told his guards to have a bit of fun. The other two ladies had not dared to argue after that, had accepted their unfortunate fate. The drinks followed, fine brandy, several shots of Averna.

That's when the change happened.

"What is Kola paying you?" Messi had asked. "You don't need to tell me the exact amount, just a ballpark figure," he'd added.

Shehu shifted uncomfortably in his seat. Money wasn't a subject that he wanted to discuss with a customer, knowing that this would probably lead to discussions on pricing, profit margins and the rest. He hesitated, took a sip of his drink.

"Don't tell me," the Italian continued without waiting for an answer. "I have a good idea anyway, and I'm sure that it's anyway performance related, bonuses for exceeding expected turnover and all of that." He also sipped on his drink, back on the brandy. He swirled the amber spirit around his teeth, feeling the warm glow of it. "Whatever it is, I can agree to give you more," he continued. "The mark-ups here in Italy are immense. We could come to some sort of arrangement. You could be paid twice even."

Concerned as he was, Shehu couldn't help but to be interested. Money was money. "How?" he asked softly.

"You can do the bidding of Kola, bring the people, drugs, booze, cigars, whatever he instructs you to sell to me. Then you could add extras of your own. You know where to get the ladies, who sells your boss his products." He shrugged. "Who'd know?" he asked.

Shehu considered the offer silently, knowing that the man was right. He had his own sources too, people from the surrounding villages that would happily supply him women, dealers who would sell him more drugs, alcohol, whatever.

"And you would buy the extra product?" he quizzed. "All of it?"

The Pig frowned. "Yes and no," he replied. "We would need to agree to the extras, agree to the pricing. But if you can get things for the right money, I have enough market over here to make it work."

"And what is the right price?" the Albanian asked. He had to be careful here, knew the margins that Kola put on things, didn't want to betray that to Il Porco.

"Let's say you trim five percent off the prices your man is getting. It still means you have the potential to make a lot of money."

It did, Shehu knew. And if he was taking the ladies from really poor areas, he could also possibly buy them for much less than his organisation was now paying. "I need to think about it," he said, the words coming out slowly, each one considered before verbalising it.

The Pig raised his glass, toasting the Albanian. "I wouldn't expect an answer tonight," he replied. "Take your thoughts home, check what is possible with your potential suppliers. When you come next time, give me your answer." He moved his glass towards Shehu, forcing him to replicate the gesture. "Cheers."

The Albanian picked up his glass, saluted the Italian. It wasn't a commitment, but it was a halfway house. He was teetering on the edge of double crossing the Albanian Mafia.

It was dangerous, but it was also an opportunity that wasn't likely to come his way again.

Gianluigi watched the speedboat move away from the jetty, manoeuvre itself onto a course to exit the harbour.

The Albanian gangster seemed to enjoy staying with Il Porco, and if rumours were to be believed, he was getting 'special' treatment from the SCU leader. As a part of his job, Gianluigi was often one of the escorts when the girls were moved from the main house to be abused on the streets, and the broken women he saw leaving the place were very different from the young hopefuls he watched arriving in the port.

He sighed, hating the job he had to do.

As an undercover agent, Gianluigi needed to blend in with the gang. He had to fight with them, kill with them, display the same outward feelings that they showed. Not to do so was a death warrant for himself. It was difficult to accept this type of behaviour, but he hoped that one day, his work would end some of the suffering. His masters weren't after the small fry – they wanted to break-up the gangs, and that meant severing the snake's head, not the tip of its tail.

He looked on as the fast boat disappeared beyond the harbour wall, his work finished for the day. It was time to call London, to report in.

He was living a lie, a lie that could easily get him killed if he was found out. And the longer he lived the double life, the more chance there was of that happening. It wasn't a job for the faint hearted, and he could feel that the stress of the situation was slowly getting to him.

Gianluigi sighed, carefully coiling the length of rope that had held the launch in place and then leaving for the day.

Into Temptation

Janet landed at King Shaka International in Durban from Johannesburg just after lunchtime, collecting her hire car from the Avis desk. She knew that either Alex or Nkosi would happily have collected her, but today she wanted to come and go as she pleased, not be tied to someone else.

The work with her people in Jo'burg was done, her agent there having completed his verbal update on the risks in South Africa and its surrounding countries. Little had changed – local politics was simply wrought with corruption; the Chinese were still investing for their future in local infrastructure projects, the returns generally coming in the form of mineral rights, whether coal, platinum, gold, or oil, it didn't really matter. These people played the long game. Spend a little now and reel it in for the next few decades. It was a pity that her own government didn't think the same way, she thought. The UK's economy had been in a state of collapse since before Brexit, and things didn't look to be improving. China might appear to be a dictatorship but having that continuity of leadership allowed it to focus past the next general election, unlike the British.

She pushed the thought from her mind, knowing that it was never going to change in her lifetime.

Finding her hire car in the nearby parking lot, she loaded her hand baggage into the boot. If all went well, she'd be back here tomorrow. A lot was hanging on how things went tonight. It was going to be all about how Alex reacted to her suggestions.

First though, she needed to do the social part of her visit and pay her respects to Kaya and Nkosi. Alex would probably be present, but she would avoid the business part of the trip until she'd got him alone. What she was about to suggest wouldn't go down too well with Andile's sister, nor with the Zulu SAS man.

What she wanted Alex to do was to even up the scores with the Albanian Mafia. It was basically a suicide mission, an operation that would be totally deniable by the British government, meaning no support from his old unit. Apart from the single asset she had in Puglia, Alex was going to be on his own.

Janet sipped on the Rooibos tea that Kaya had prepared for them all, trying to keep things light, very aware that the girl had lost her last direct family member because of the work that her brother-in-law was a part of. She glanced over at Alex, wasn't overly surprised that he was watching her, not his sister-in-law. He wasn't the leader of the SAS because he was stupid – he'd no doubt already guessed that she was here on a mission, not just to pass on her sympathies.

"You'll be staying for some food?" Kaya asked, noticing the glance towards Alex. "Or do you have other business that needs attention?"

Janet pulled her eyes back to the Zulu girl, annoyed that she'd been caught out so easily. "Let me take you all out," she offered. "My treat."

"That's not necessary," Nkosi said. "The kids have school tomorrow, so eating out is difficult." He glanced at his brother-in-law, sensed his need to talk to Janet alone. "You can have a bite to eat here, then maybe yourself and Alex can go and have a quiet drink and a catch-up. I'm certain that you have things to discuss."

Janet nodded, feeling slightly cornered.

"I've got a better idea," Alex cut in. "Why don't Janet and myself go and grab some food and bring it back here. We can grab a drink while we wait for things to be ready, and you can get the kids ready for bed."

"That would be great," Kaya agreed. "I wasn't really expecting to feed you all, and it is school tomorrow. A late night wouldn't be great for them."

Janet and Alex left the house soon afterwards, a food order at the ready.

"We don't need to rush too much," Alex said as he pointed his car towards the centre of Umhlanga Rocks. "Give the kids a chance to get off to sleep." He stopped, waiting for a second to see if the Six lady would say something. When nothing came, he went on. "I guess that you're not only here to give Kaya commiserations for the loss of her sister." It was out there, and he realised just how harsh it sounded. "I'm sorry. That was unkind."

Janet stared ahead, watching the road, considering her response. "But you're pretty much right," she eventually replied. She finally looked across the car at the SAS colonel. "I did want her to know that we all cared deeply for Andile, that she was a friend, but no, that's not the main reason for my visit." She looked back out of the car windscreen. "I came to see how you were coping, to see if you had plans to return."

Alex pursed his lips, considering the statement.

"I'm not sure yet," he replied softly. "I'm not certain that my head's in the right place. I'd probably be doing things for me, not for the good of my country. That might just put others in danger."

Janet gave the smallest of nods, fairly certain that she understood Alex's feelings. "Revenge is a dish best served cold," she replied softly. "And I guess you want to get the people that killed Andile and the kids." She paused, knew the answer already.

Alex glanced across, slowing the car and pulling into the side of the road. "Yes, but not if it will endanger others," he allowed.

Janet had considered how best to tell Alex what she now knew, had run different scenarios in her head. Now she realised that the only way was to be direct, to give him the facts that she had discovered so far. She drew a deep breath and started.

"We have an agent in Italy, a man who has worked his way into the ranks of the Sacra Corona Unita down in Puglia. We want him to identify the main players down there, to find out who is pulling the strings. We want to shut down all of their operations there, not to just close down one channel. They are dealing drugs, girls, cigarettes, alcohol. They have the area in their pockets, the local police force paid to turn a blind eye. We are working with the national police people to try and stop this."

"Is that the Carabinieri?" Alex asked.

"Not really, though they may get involved. We are mainly working with the Guardia di Finanza, the national body that fights drug trafficking, money laundering, smuggling, illegal immigration, amongst other things. The Carabinieri are interlinked with them, but they have more of a military leaning."

"Okay," Alex replied, not overly interested in the details. "But what's this got to do with me? You've already mentioned a link to the Puglia region when you named this Shehu character, though you gave me no other details."

"One of the main suppliers of both drugs and people to the SCU is the Albanian Mafia. They work hand-in-hand, the Albanians running a route for drugs coming from Afghanistan, and also for girls from eastern Europe, including from their own country."

Alex was now fully focussed on the MI6 chief, the Albanian connection getting his total attention.

"Soon after the death of Andile and the kids, the leader of the Albanians in the UK returned to his country in a bit of a hurry. Whether the two things are connected, we're not a hundred percent certain, but we believe that they are. It seems that he was recalled, perhaps overstepping the mark in the eyes of his superiors. As you know, that's Shehu."

Alex switched off the ignition. "When you gave me his name you were still researching him. Is it confirmed that he killed my wife?" he asked coldly.

"We're still digging, but we believe that he at least ordered it," Janet replied. "You were the SAS top dog, and that in his eyes would have meant you were responsible for the damage done to his organisation." She paused, considering her next words. "He was killing our boys in blue, we used you and the team to protect the police, and soon after that Andile and the kids are dead. Then he is recalled to Tirana if we're right. Too many coincidences for me."

Alex nodded. "So he's definitely back at home in Albania. Do we know where?"

Janet nodded. "He's being used to supply drugs, girls, whatever, to the Sacra Corona Unita. Our man in Brindisi sees him almost every week. It seems he's quite chummy with the local SCU chief." She paused. "Some of this you're already aware of, but we've now obtained more detail, checked out some of the facts."

"Why are you telling me all of this?" Alex asked. He thought that he could guess why, but he needed to hear it from her.

"I didn't expect you to be ready to return to the Regiment yet, but I guessed that you would be keen to get to the man who killed your family," the spy replied. "I would also like to see him removed, both for professional and personal reasons. He badly hurt our police force, and he killed someone that I was pleased to consider a friend." Over the years, Janet had spent a lot of time with Alex's wife. "I wondered if you were ready to return to duty, even if it wasn't yet with the SAS."

Alex looked over at the MI6 leader, trying to read her thoughts. "I think that you know me well enough to know the answer to your questions. One day, I will avenge my family's deaths, with or without the help of the British government," he stated.

Janet coloured slightly, knowing that her next statement was going to go down badly. "This would be without the help of the government," she stated. "Or at least officially without their help."

Alex shook his head, frustration showing on his face. "So this is a deniable operation?" he asked.

Janet nodded, wondering if it was fair to ask her friend and colleague to risk his life without having any support from the UK military. Against that, she knew she was offering the man a chance of revenge, however suicidal that chance might prove to be. "I will help where I can, but on the face of it, you'd be on your own."

Alex stared ahead, then switched on the car engine.

"The others will be waiting, so we'd better get on with things." He pulled away, heading towards the town centre. "Not a word of this to Nkosi," he warned the spy chief. "I can't have him volunteering to join this bloody madness. He's still lucky enough to have a family."

As soon as he said it, he knew that it was unfair. Janet hadn't killed his family. She was just giving him a chance to do what he wanted to do anyway. To get revenge for Andile and the kids.

The evening had been a tense affair following their exchange on the way to get the food, Janet certain that Nkosi and Kaya had picked up on it. She caught the Zulu glancing at his brother-in-law far too often, clearly aware of his change in mood, though neither he nor his wife asked any questions. Perhaps they were used to it since the death of Andile, Janet decided.

She'd left early, pleased to get back to her small hotel, to have a nightcap alone. Her plane was leaving the following evening, an Emirates flight via Dubai. After winding down over a cognac, she decided on a second brandy, no need to rush to bed, her mission as complete as possible for now. She had planted her seed and now it was up to Alex to make a decision. That might take some time.

The Six lady had been about to call it a night when the door to the small bar area opened at just after ten. She glanced over, expecting to see another hotel guest.

Alex stood in the doorway, his facial expression tight like a mask. He looked as though he may have been crying, something that Janet had never witnessed over all the time she had known the man.

"A beer?" she asked as he walked over to where she sat.

He nodded, took a seat close to her, did a sweep of the room, making certain that there was no-one close enough to eavesdrop. "We need to talk," he said quietly.

It was obvious what the conversation was going to be about, and Janet wondered if her room might be a better place for it to take place. A bit of privacy to say what needed to be said. "You've already made your decision?" she asked, deciding to go with the flow. The place was almost empty, just a touristy looking couple on the far side of the room, the barman cleaning up behind his bar.

Alex nodded, looked towards the bar.

Janet got out of her seat, ordered a beer and a third brandy. She was going to sleep well, that was for sure. She carried the drinks over to their corner. "You don't need to rush, you know," she said. "I'm leaving tomorrow evening. Sleep on it if you want."

The SAS colonel shook his head. "I think you knew my answer before you left Babylon-on-Thames," he stated, using the nickname for the SIS London headquarters. "Maybe you knew it even before that."

Janet nodded. "What happened to your family was disgusting. You only want to do what any of us would wish to do, to take some kind of revenge." She paused. "The only difference is, most of us wouldn't know where to start to get it."

Alex took a large gulp of the Castle beer, put the glass down on the table. He nodded. "How do we play it?" he asked.

The MI6 chief steepled her fingers, her plan still only half-hatched. "As I said earlier, officially you'd be on your own, a rogue agent. Covertly I will help, but it will only be through my man in Brindisi. He will be our eyes and ears on the ground. As I said earlier, he sees Luan Shehu most weeks, even though he is working for the Italians. Shehu seems to be the direct link between SCU and the Albanian Mafia, the man who is charged with supplying whatever Sacra Corona needs. He is the conduit between the two organisations."

"Does your man have an idea of how I could isolate the Albanian?"

Janet decided not to ask why isolating Shehu was important. "No. He isn't aware of this idea yet. And anyway, I think that things like that will be best left to you when you're on the ground."

"Will I receive financial support? Weapons?"

A nod from the MI6 lady. "I will discreetly organise some funding, more than enough for travel, hotels, and the rest. Not payment, but let's call it 'expenses plus'. Gianluigi will look into weapons once you're in Italy."

"I'll be going to Italy, not Albania?"

"I have no assets in Albania. The mafia there is tight, clan-like. Unless you are family, then you're out. We need to do things from across the water."

Alex nodded. One man in support was better than none. Transport and communication in Italy was far better than that in Albania. It was the right place to start. Later... well, only time would tell.

"When do I go?"

Janet let out a long breath, her plan now a step further along. She had her weapon, a highly trained soldier with a massive grudge against her target. "Soon," she replied. "Let me think about that overnight," she added. "Can we meet tomorrow?"

Alex finished his beer, nodded. "I can be here for nine."

Janet stood, her glass still only half empty. "I'll have something more concrete by then," she said. "A few calls tonight, and we'll know when's good to move. Sleep well."

Falling Together

Rumours were getting through to Kola that his star salesman was spending far too much time with his customers, much more than was necessary to service an established and well-oiled marketplace. It had happened before with others, and he had no doubt that it would happen again: good people were always in demand, and he had no doubt that his old mate Messi would be angling for something. It was all about how to handle it.

His meeting with Shehu was scheduled for thirty minutes time. He reflected on how he'd handled similar situations in the past. A warning was often sufficient, though he'd also had one man killed for trying to take a cut of the family's earnings. Which route would be best for the present transgressor?

Shehu had done a great job in the UK, boosted profits, and opened new markets there. He'd also overstepped the mark, taken the war to the authorities over there. And here he was again, doing so well, but pressing for more.

Was it time to dispose of him? It was the simplest route. He'd already given the man a subtle warning.

He looked at the firm's present income streams, both in the Italian operation and the one in the UK, could easily spot the trends. The trade with Italy was up; the trend in London was down, ever since Shehu had been withdrawn from the market. The cause was obvious – the man was good at what he did.

Should he directly contact Il Porco, warn him to back-off? Would that ruin the trade, cause the Italian to look elsewhere for his goods?

Kill Il Porco? Another possibility, but possibly the end of that market. Plus a war with the SCU. That could be costly.

Whatever he was to do had to directly affect Luan Shehu. He was the man endangering the business. He was the man that had to be stopped, possibly terminally.

An idea was forming in his head. A possibility that would put a stop to the suspected skimming of his profits, stop his man from switching sides, but keep the Sacra Corona in his pocket.

Gianluigi had noticed a pattern emerging. The Albanian had usually arrived on random dates, sometimes weekend, sometimes midweek. There had seemed to be no rhyme nor reason as to why, but London had asked him to record the visits, noting the day, dates, and duration. The man was getting a lot of interest from the people in Vauxhall.

Initially, the man's arrival had been sporadic, sometimes more than once a week, sometimes not for two or three. He usually left the same day, just passing on the goods he'd brought to the relevant people in Sacra Corona Unita, then getting out of the country. To an Intelligence Officer, that made sense. The man was not officially meant to be in Italy, did not register his presence with any sort of border control, didn't pass his goods through any customs authority.

And that also made sense.

But things had changed. The Albanian was now in Brindisi almost every Friday, leaving on Saturday, sometimes Sunday. He was spending all of his time in the country with Mister Messi, not visiting the people who were actually dealing the produce on the ground.

And he was bringing in more goods than before, especially women.

London seemed pleased when this information was passed back to them. They liked patterns, liked predictability. And now they were getting it.

"Is there some way that you can confirm what the two men get up to on their Friday evening meetings?" his handler had asked. Gianluigi had already reported the rumours, the fact that The Pig and The Albanian were sampling the goods, and not just the girls.

"Not really," he admitted. "Access to the villa is tightly controlled, only trusted veterans selected to do duties there. The old man is a suspicious bastard, doesn't like new folk. He sees everyone as a possible infiltrator."

"So no way to see what is happening first hand?"

Gianluigi frowned. Asking too many questions and pressing too hard would put him at risk. "It took me a long time to get this far," he reminded London. "I don't want people to start questioning my loyalties."

There was a lengthy silence at the other end of the phone. The Italian thought he could hear a conversation, as if someone had their hand over the microphone, his handler getting a second opinion on something. He used the quiet to listen to his own surroundings, making certain that he wasn't being monitored in some way, that no-one was close by.

The MI6 handler finally came back. "Keep doing what you are doing," he said. "Be careful not to raise the SCU peoples suspicions." Again, another voice in the background. "We hope to have someone join you in a few days. They will need a full briefing, not just about the SCU boss, but also about the activities of the Albanian."

"Another Italian?" the agent asked. "Is he safe?"

"Not an Italian," London replied. "An Englishman, ex-military." It was not one hundred percent true, but it was close enough. Alex was still with the Special Air Service, but accepting this mission might well be the end of that.

In all probability, it would be the end altogether. This was a suicide mission.

"We are seeing a pattern emerging," Janet said to Alex, her cell phone secure, but his not so. It meant that he had to be careful how he replied, to make sure that he limited his questions, kept things obscure. "Our mark seems to have become quite predictable."

"Does this mean we are good to go?" the SAS man asked.

Janet bit her lower lip, sincerely hoping that she wasn't about to send a good man to his maker. The chances of the Italians or Albanians having monitoring services that would capture the call were miniscule, but they were still there. And anyway, the Americans, Russians, or Chinese might pick something up, sell it on for future favours. That was the big problem in the spying game: no-one trusted anyone.

"Yes," she finally agreed. "I've made a bank transfer to you already. And you know where you need to go," she continued. "I will send details of your rendezvous point once you are on the ground."

Alex had already planned his options for the trip down to Brindisi, just needed the green light. "Do I travel as me?" he asked, knowing that may be unwise. If someone joined the dots and clocked him as a senior man in the special forces, then any freedom of movement would go out of the window.

"You'll have a delivery tomorrow," Janet replied. "It will have everything you need." Alex guessed that this meant a new ID, a passport, a background story, or legend. It was something that the Secret Intelligence Service were good at. Hiding the truth.

"I'll text to confirm receipt, then let you know my travel dates by a mix of email and texts." He'd done this sort of thing before, breaking up messages when he had no secure comms, making it more difficult for any digital eavesdropper to put things together. "We can talk again once I'm in place," he finished.

"Good luck," Janet said. She pressed the red button on her phone, cutting the connection.

The project was rolling.

"I'm offering you a promotion Luan," Kola said, a smile on his face.

"Promotion?"

"Yes. I've reviewed your results, and I want you to look into the rest of our imports into the Italian markets. Use Brindisi as a role model. It means more travel to other ports up and down the east coast of the country, but if we get the same returns from the other operations, you will get your rewards too." Kola watched his man's face as he laid out the plan. He thought that he noticed a slight wince, a blink of the eyes, as if Shehu had heard something that he hadn't wanted to hear.

"Right," the man had replied after a moment's hesitation. "When do you want this to happen?" Shehu knew there was no way out. You can't just walk away from the mafia. That is a certain death sentence.

"Find a lieutenant, do a handover with your main contacts. I'd like things to start soon," the senior man added. He noted that Shehu wasn't able to look into his eyes, a likely sign of a hidden secret. "The sooner the better," he said. "If we can up the profits in the rest of the supply chains, then we will be in a great position to reward you well." A carrot, to help smooth out the losses, Kola thought. And besides, this was a better solution to having his golden goose killed off.

The mafia boss gave his man a broad smile. "I hope that you're happy with this?" he asked. "It's another step up the ladder."

"I appreciate your confidence in me," Shehu replied, knowing that there really was no other possible answer. Sometimes you simply had to make the best out of a bad situation. "I will do my best."

Basri Kola was fairly sure that Luan Shehu would do just that. He was also sure that his man knew the alternatives. And that he had been terribly close to meeting with one of them.

"Good."

"The Englishman will arrive tomorrow evening," the MI6 handler informed his man on the ground. "Details are not certain right now. He's organising his own transport."

"How will I find him?" Gianluigi asked. He was nervous. Someone he didn't know coming into his territory. Someone who knew the truth about him.

"We should agree a time and place that the two of you can meet."

The Italian considered where that place should be. Somewhere that no-one would see him, somewhere away from Brindisi if possible. He couldn't risk being seen with an outsider, especially a foreigner with a military background. A foreigner with connections to the Secret Intelligence Service. "Let me think about it," he replied, buying himself a little time. "It needs to be somewhere safe," he added. Safe for himself.

Back in London, the MI6 man nodded. He would have given a similar reply. Operating alone and undercover was a tough existence. Giving up your name to someone you didn't know was tougher.

"That's fine," he replied. "You have about twenty-four hours to decide on the right place," he added.

"I'll mail you my decision in good time," Gianluigi said. "Our usual code."

'Keep safe," the Six man said, signing off. He wondered again if the Chief's idea was the right one. It had taken over a year for the Italian police to infiltrate a man into the Sacra Corona Unita's ranks, and if any of this went wrong, that year of work would be wasted. He pursed his lips, considering what else he could do to protect his shared asset, came up with no new ideas. "Keep safe," he muttered to himself this time.

Not doing so was not worth thinking about.

Shehu knew that he had dodged a bullet, didn't really understand how. He understood exactly how his organisation worked, knew that crossing them in any way was suicidal. He had done it and lived to tell the tale. Okay, he had lost some of his newfound 'privileges', but in his new role he would possibly be exposed to even more. He wasn't involved in one supply route now, but to many. And each one could be exploited.

He grinned to himself, trying to put a positive spin on things, but somewhere deep in his brain he still had a nagging doubt. Why had Kola allowed him to continue? Why was he not lying in some rock quarry, his body being devoured by the birds and rodents?

Business was booming with Brindisi, and he had played a major part in that. If he hadn't agreed to his side-line with Il Porco, then the turnover figures would have been even higher.

"It's time to stop," he warned himself. He had been lucky, now he needed to be careful. And anyway, Kola had basically promised him a share in the profits. His star was shining brightly. It was not a time to take unnecessary risks.

Enemy Territory

There was no easy way to get from Durban to Puglia. It was a twisted trip, and the best option to Alex was to use Emirates that flew directly from his new home city to Dubai, then to use the same people to get him to Rome. From there it was a choice of a seven hour drive, or a one hour flight with ITA Airways to put him at his destination. He took the simple option and flew.

Papola Casale Airport was nothing spectacular, but by the time he arrived there, Alex was just pleased to be out of aeroplanes. Including flight connection times he'd been on the go for almost twenty-four hours, and all he wanted now was a shower and a sleep.

He approached the Avis car hire desk, his ride already booked from South Africa. An Alfa Romeo Giulia was awaiting his collection, not a spectacular motor, but also nothing conspicuous. A car in a million. Just what he wanted.

He sat in the vehicle, switched on his mobile phone. A message was waiting.

Portico of the Templars 2000 hours was all that it said. Alex glanced at his watch. Two o'clock, giving him six hours to get his act together, get a little rest, and get an idea of the layout of the city.

How will I know who I'm meeting? he typed on his touch screen.

Thirty seconds later the answer came. *He will know you.*

Alex put the phone away, pursed his lips. He didn't like the thought of a meeting that he had little or no control over, but there again, he could understand that the person he was to meet would be nervous. Working undercover is stressful, and no doubt the agent would be watching him closely before revealing himself. Just because Six said Alex was a good guy wouldn't be enough. The man would want to make certain that he hadn't inadvertently brought others to the meet.

Starting the car, Alex tapped his hotel details into the satnav. First things first. Let's find a bed, and then a little later a map of the city. He had time and being rested meant being alert.

Gianluigi watched the Brit from the shadows of the cathedral as he warily crossed the Piazza Duomo, making his way towards the Portico of the Templars. His decision to use the place was because it rang with a bit of history – the reference to the Knights Templar would possibly pique the British man's interests, even though the ex-palace had nothing to do with them. It was just a label the building had picked-up from back in the eighteenth century, though the sand and white coloured stonework was now just a front to a much more modern museum.

It wasn't the type of place he'd originally planned to meet, but it was an area that was easy for an outsider to find, a part of the old town close to the harbour area with many tourist attractions. It meant that the Englishman wouldn't stand out in a crowd, especially now in the early evening. The streets weren't full, but there was at least a flow of people here, many of them foreigners.

He looked on as the man made a pass of the building, stopping briefly to study the architecture, taking his phone out and taking a few pictures.

Very professional, the Italian man thought. Pretending to be just another tourist while all the time quietly scanning his surroundings, checking for anything or anyone out of the ordinary. A man after his own heart.

He stayed in his place, the meeting time still twelve minutes away. No point in rushing. They were going to get to know each other soon enough.

Alex spotted a slight movement across the square from the rendezvous point, guessed it was likely to be his contact. He continued his scan of the area, taking a couple of photographs to keep appearing to be the visitor that he was supposed to be. He wouldn't approach the man, would wait for him to come over, following the instructions in his messages. In the meantime he would continue his own checks, making certain that he hadn't been followed from his nearby hotel.

He knew from experience that complacency was deadly. Check everything, then do it all again. And if time permitted, again.

He crossed the square, looked into a small café, read the menu, and walked away as if he'd decided against it. He turned, retraced his steps, a sure way to catch out someone tailing him too closely.

Nothing.

He moved back to the Portico of the Templars. It was almost eight o'clock. Time to meet a stranger.

Gianluigi stepped out of his secret observation position, tailed the Brit for the final minute, hanging back about forty metres, doing a final check that no-one else was monitoring the two of them.

Again nothing.

He put an inch to his step, easily closing the gap on Alex Green. The man looked every bit the tourist, sauntering along without a care in the world, pausing for pictures, arriving once more in front of the Portico of the Templars at exactly eight.

"Alex Green?" he enquired, verifying what he already knew.

The man turned to face him, nodding. "You must be Gianluigi," he replied quietly. "Where do you want to go? My hotel?"

The Italian shook his head, pointed to the corner of the square. "I have my car behind the cathedral," he said. "And the SCU monitor the hotels. Tourists like the ladies and are easy to blackmail afterwards. Be careful."

Alex guessed that his contact knew nothing about his wife's murder, the fact that a woman was the last thing on his mind. "Thanks." In time, perhaps he would explain to his host what drove him, but for now, he just wanted to see what the man could offer. The Secret Intelligence Service generally worked on a 'need-to-know' basis, and Janet and her team had probably given the Italian only the bare essentials. SOP. Standard Operating Procedure.

They walked in silence across the Piazza, both still unobtrusively checking their surroundings, looking for tell-tale indications that things were not right.

Gianluigi pulled out his car fob, pressing the unlocking button as they approached a small Fiat. "We'll drive out of town, somewhere private."

Alex nodded silently, saving his words. He knew what it was like to be in situations that were not of your choosing. Danger was a part of the job, but that didn't make it any easier.

He remained silent as Gianluigi expertly guided the small car out of the city centre, his driving that of a local. Talk would come soon enough.

They passed the airport, driving along Via di Torre Testa, the sea on the right of the car. Not far past the end of the runway, Gianluigi pulled off onto a dirt track into an untarmacked parking area, deserted at this hour. There was one road in, the same road out. No chance of a disturbance without them both being aware of it.

The Italian switched off the engine, turned out the lights. "This should be safe enough," he said. They could hear the waves breaking on the rocks below them, but apart from that, the place was peaceful. "Can I ask why you are here?"

Alex opened his car door. "Let's walk," he replied. A car could be bugged, and anyhow, the evening was still warm.

The Italian got out and locked the car, understanding. "So Vauxhall gave you my name at least," he stated. "Did they tell you what I'm doing here?"

"That you're making your way into the SCU, infiltrating their ranks. I guess that sometime in the future they'll want to use that to break-up the drug gangs, the other rackets that Sacra Corona are involved in. I don't think that Six can do that alone, so I also guess that they are working with the Italian Police, that you must be involved with the local cops."

Gianluigi grimaced, the light of the moon making the expression clear to Alex even in the darkness. "Not the local cops," he said bitterly. "They are as bad as some of the gangsters. I am with the national police, though I haven't been in a uniform for over four years now."

Alex studied the man, trying to get a feel for him. "That's a long time to be living a lie," he offered. "No family, I guess?"

The Italian nodded, his face tight. "My wife died around six years back. Drugs. I made it my job to do anything in my power to help here in the fight against them. And here in Brindisi that means bringing down the SCU."

Alex paused, fully understanding the man's pain. "Let me tell you my story," he finally suggested. "Then I think you'll understand what I have to do too."

They spent the next thirty-five minutes sharing one another's sorry tales, then a further hour talking about what Gianluigi had been reporting back to the people in London that he'd been seconded to. "By the way, just call me Gian," he told Alex as the clock approached ten. "I don't know why my mother gave me what amounts to two names, but most people just use the first of them. I guess it's easier for you, more like 'Jan' in English."

The SAS man nodded. "Jan was a common name when I was based down in Plymouth with the Marines," he told his newfound friend. "It was also a nickname for the locals." He'd already explained his route to the top of the elite Regiment, how he'd started at the very bottom and worked his way up. "So where do we go from here?" he asked.

Gianluigi looked towards the road as a car roared past, fairly certain that the two of them were well out of sight. "Today's Wednesday," he started. "Which means we have two days before your target will be here." He hesitated, considering the wisdom of his next words. "I could run you down to the city again, show you The Pig's villa. It would give you an idea of what we're up against."

"What I'm up against," Alex corrected him.

"If you're against Sacra Corona, then I'm with you."

Alex frowned. He needed all the help he could get, but dragging in an undercover cop wasn't a part of the plan. "And you say that Shehu should be here again on Friday?"

"He's been here the last four in a row, as I said. Him and Il Porco have their fun, then he gets himself back to Albania in the morning."

"Fun," Alex said flatly. "Not for the poor buggers that are getting raped."

"I couldn't agree more. I see them the morning after when their futures are already mapped out. God knows how long they can last. Some of them are just bloody kids."

They had returned to the car, sat perched on the bonnet. "Do you think I could take Shehu out in only two days' time?"

Gianluigi puckered his lips, thinking about the proposal. "I think you should see the layout first, see what the man does while he's here. Then you have a full week to make a plan, to organise how you want to do it. We still need to get equipment together, weapons, anything else you need." He looked towards the moon, looking for inspiration. "Then we also need a plan to get you out of here in one piece."

Alex hadn't thought that far ahead. He wanted to avenge the deaths of his family, and if he escaped that, then so be it. If not... He decided it was best not to tell the Italian any of this. A suicidal special forces operative wasn't the company an undercover policeman would wish for. "If I take out Shehu, do you also want The Pig gone too?" he asked, changing the subject.

Gianluigi gave a very slow nod, as if he hadn't considered this possibility up to now. "I'm not sure my masters would agree to that," he allowed. "They want a bigger fish, the very top of the leadership ladder."

"You said that Messi is the top man for this region, the main man for Sacra Corona Unita. Surely taking him down – plus the man heading his supply route - would be a major coup for the authorities? Leave the SCU headless and without product to sell."

The Italian thought it through, a silence descending between the two men.

"They might buy it," he said eventually.

"I could ask London to pressure them, sell it as a chance in a lifetime. Who knows, it might really be that anyway."

Gianluigi stood, Alex following suit. "Let me show you the villa first. Then we can discuss our options." The local walked to his car door. "But in answer to your question – yes, I would love to kill Il Porco."

It was almost eleven o'clock before they reached the villa. Alex was tired from all of the travel, knowing that Gian was right. Rushing things to satisfy his own appetite was putting both men at terrible risk. Doing proper surveillance and understanding what he was up against was the right way forward. Cocking up and becoming another dead body was no use to anyone.

Gianluigi parked the car almost three hundred metres from the building's outer wall, far enough so as not to alarm anyone patrolling the grounds. He knew that the gatehouse was normally not manned, the security cameras and movement sensors doing the work of a guard. Inside, those same sensors would trigger an alarm, allowing a security man to view the monitors, to assess from a safe distance what the threat was.

Outside, two dog handlers and their Dobermans patrolled the gardens, both in radio contact with the control room. During the day the dogs were kennelled, the handlers on call.

"During the day the grounds are patrolled by SCU guards," Gian explained as he led Alex to a place above the property and explained the security set-up. "They are armed with both MP5s and handguns. I'm not sure how many others are housed within the place."

Alex viewed the villa, guessing that it must have around ten bedrooms, God knows how many other rooms. A swimming pool sat below a vast balcony, below that a steep cliff that fell all of the way to the sea. From where he stood, an approach from the water looked all but impossible.

"How would you get in?" he asked.

"I'd be tempted not to bother," the Italian replied. "I think that I'd aim to take The Pig out when he was away from the place. The only problem with that is, he doesn't telegraph his trips. And he doesn't do business on the outside without a team of thugs being with him."

"So planning something away from the property is almost impossible without serious support," the SAS man surmised.

"We could take out Shehu down at the docks. He'd be alone then."

Alex considered the option. "But then you lose your target," he finally said. "If the Albanian is killed, then Messi will increase his security, make a difficult job even more so."

"Very true."

"So the only way to do this is to take them down at the same time. And that would mean on one of their nights together."

"I'd say that you're right," Gian conceded.

"So somehow we need to get inside the villa." Alex studied the property's perimeter wall, guessed it to be around two metres in height. To get in, that would first need to be crossed, somehow without being ripped apart by a Doberman Pinscher, and then making it to the building itself while avoiding CCTV and other sensors that he was certain criss-crossed the grounds. Inside they would be working blind, unsure of the villa's layout, of where the two targets were housed, of whether other guards were based in there.

He shook his head, alert but exhausted.

"Let's call it a night," he said, stifling a yawn. "I'll come back tomorrow, spy out the land in daylight. Try and form a plan."

Gianluigi nodded his agreement. "I've been waiting for years, so another week will not be too long." He yawned, the tiredness infectious. "I can't be with you tomorrow, but we can meet again in the evening."

Alex began to trudge thoughtfully back towards the Fiat. "I can find the spot we were at earlier this evening," he said. "I can meet you there and we can compare notes."

"Take care Alex Green," Gianluigi said in a whispered warning. "These are dangerous times, and Sacra Corona are dreadfully violent people. They will be merciless." He ran a finger across his throat to reinforce the message. "If we are caught, we will die."

"The Regiment's motto is 'Who Dares Wins'," the SAS man replied. "Let me look and think things through. We will find a way."

Poking The Pig

In daylight the villa looked beautiful, it's position directly above the cliffs making it look more like a fortress, dominating the choppy sea below. The walls were a brilliant white, the window frames and balcony black, the twenty metre horizon pool an azure blue before the dramatic steep drop off down to the Mediterranean Sea.

It was eight o'clock in the morning and Alex had parked his car four hundred metres away from the building, the place where all the nearby housing basically stopped. It gave him few places to try and observe the target without being exposed to watchers from the house. There was a smattering of trees, a couple of spiky gorse bushes, little to use as a makeshift observation post, or an OP in military speak. Il Porco and his people had done their homework, chosen well. Getting close to them without being noticed would not be easy.

Alex pulled on a baseball cap, deciding to walk by the villa, get a better feel for his options. The cap would keep the already warm sun off his face, but also disguise his identity a little from CCTV and the villa guards. To anyone watching, he intended to be seen as just another nosy tourist, someone looking to see how the other half lived.

There was one road in, one road out. It was the same one he'd driven along the previous night with Gian. He set off along it, deciding that making a track across the rocky terrain that formed the no-man's-land was just going to attract too much attention. This wasn't going to be easy.

Twenty metres from the main gate, he halted, turned towards the sea. From a small day pack he pulled out a camera, pointed it towards the water. Going closer was out of the question. His image would be stored in the building's CCTV system, then computers there would use it to pick him out if he made a return journey.

He stepped towards the Adriatic, deciding that this is just what a visitor would do. He was northwest of the villa, close to a part of the wall that topped the cliff edge. Was this a possible way in? He took a couple of photos, zooming in on places that might be climbable. There weren't many.

A car passed along the road behind him, paused as the targets gates swung open. He risked a glimpse back, again as a tourist might do, trying to see who was rich enough to live in such a place.

A black Mercedes Metris edged through the gates, windows as dark as the paintwork. It was the sort of van you'd use if you didn't want people to know who or what was inside. Great for transporting illegal material, people who weren't officially there. The gates closed behind it, shutting out the view of the grounds.

It gave Alex only about forty seconds to observe the contents of the villa walls, not much, but enough to pick out a few things.

Distance from gate to house, approximately two hundred metres.

Armed guards patrolling the grounds, weapons slung lazily across their backs. One man had been at the gate, possibly ordered there to check the delivery was as expected.

No sign of the kennels. Possibly around the back of the villa.

No dogs, just as Gianluigi had said. At least for the daytime patrols.

A low wooden fence close to the building and around the pool area. Alex guessed that this was a sort of safety barrier for night-time gatherings. You wouldn't want your guests getting chewed up by the Dobermans.

No sign of cameras or IR sensors, but he suspected that there must be several. A man with the sort of money he was looking at would have the whole security package, especially in his line of work.

Alex looked again to the sea, once more the tourist, opened the pack and placed the camera back inside.

He needed to find a way to get close to the other side of the house. Even if it meant approaching over the rocky sand. There simply had to be a way, and he had a map in the car.

Time to go.

Kola had requested the meeting, a kind of progress report of sorts, a decision between life and death at the worst.

"So you've found your replacement," he said, not a question but a statement, proof that he had his finger totally on the button. "Does that mean less trips across to Brindisi, less time with that bastard The Pig?"

"Yes and yes," Shehu confirmed. "I take Fisnik over there tomorrow."

"Introductions and handover?"

Shehu nodded, not enjoying the interrogation, again wondering how much his boss actually knew. "He needs to know the people, who to depend on, who to watch out for," he said. "This is hopefully the last trip there for a while, perhaps one more next week to see how the man operates alone."

Kola narrowed his eyes, as if trying to see inside of his junior's head, to read his mind. "Good," he finally allowed. "Then you will have more time to focus on my other operations."

"That is the plan," Shehu agreed. "And you will soon see results."

They met at the same spot – an alien concept to both the Italian and the SAS man, but the only place that Alex knew outside of the city. It was dark, the time already after nine.

"It's just as you described," the Englishman said. "No simple approach, guards day and night, weapons, dogs, the lot. No easy way in."

"But it can be done?"

"Nothing is impossible," Alex stated. "We will find a way to take down the two of them. It's what they both deserve." His voice was cold, hard. "It's their time, our justice. I just need to put together a plan."

"The Albanian should be here tomorrow," Gian said. "Do you want to see him, get eyes on the target?"

Alex nodded. "That would be good."

'Come to pier seven tomorrow morning," the Italian replied. "He normally arrives around ten o'clock, but that can change depending on the weather. 'd say be there from about eight. Find a spot where you can watch the harbour entrance, see the small boats come in. His will be a fast speedboat."

Alex nodded. "I'll be there."

The call to London was after ten in Italy, nine o'clock in the UK.

"I'm going to need tools for the job," Alex told Janet over his cell phone. "I'll get a list to you over a more secure connection."

"I'll sort it out. Do everything through Gianluigi."

Alex hesitated, unsure what he could get away with over an unsecured connection. "You trust him?" he finally asked.

Janet considered her words before speaking. "I have never met him in person, and I don't think it would be wise to do so. He comes highly recommended by his own people," she allowed. More would be too much. "He has his own reasons to work with us."

Alex already understood this, knew not to say more right now.

"Do you have any idea how you will handle things yet? I guess that your shopping list is ready." The Six chief interrupted his thoughts, stopping him thinking about his own reasons for the hit. "Can everything be sourced locally?"

"Everything can be found locally, I believe, except for possibly one item," the SAS colonel replied. "I need an accurate long," he added, deciding that this should mean nothing to most people if the call was being monitored. "I'll get details for you tomorrow, but I think you understand. It's the sort of job that you need to do from a distance."

Janet got the message. Alex needed to make this kill from afar. That needed a specialist weapon.

"And it will be two jobs, not one," the soldier added.

"Two?"

"The local mark must go too. Not for me, for our Italian friend."

They broke off the connection, Alex lying back on his bed, planning his moves for the morning.

Thirteen hundred miles away, Janet Anderson wondered what sort of a war she might have just started. At the end of the day, one dead bad apple or two wasn't really an issue.

She shrugged, went through to her bedroom where Mike Sanders waited patiently for her work to finish. Tomorrow was another day.

They met again outside of the town, this time a further three miles down the coast, not letting themselves get into an obvious pattern. People noticed patterns: nature rarely repeated things as exactly as humans, and some part of a person's prehistoric mind questioned why they should happen at all. They drew attention.

"Did you see him?" Gian asked.

"I did," Alex said nodding, his features dark in the moonlight. "And he is definitely this Shehu character?"

"It's him. I've managed to get photos, had MI6 check that they match."

Alex pursed his lips into a thin line, the temptation to just smash into the villa and kill the Albanian was almost overwhelming. "I have put together a list of what we need," he finally continued.

"I have a secure cell, a SIM card that was passed to me by London," Gianluigi replied. "We can call my handler, talk things through."

"First I think that you should look through it, see what we can manage locally. Then I suggest we call the Chief together, let her decide if she can help. I have some sort of a plan, but it will only work if I can get what I need." He pulled out a small notebook, a list of less than ten items handwritten on it. "What do you think?"

The Italian policeman read through the list, flicking on the car's overhead light to so, reading swiftly. At the end, he nodded, switched off the lamp. "I can do most of it, but not all," he confirmed. "Handguns, no problem. Ropes and climbing gear, the same. A boat..." He tailed off.

"Couldn't we steal one from the harbour?"

Gian raised his eyebrows. "We could, but who would drive it?" he asked.

"The SAS have a boat troop," Alex replied. "Let me worry about that." He looked back to the road, checking that no-one had been attracted by the light. "And the last item?"

"For that one, I cannot help," Gian said shaking his head. "I'm also not sure about stealing a boat. It would attract attention."

"Then let's get on the phone," Alex replied. "It's time that Janet Anderson started earning her keep."

Janet had guessed correctly about what her man wanted, and now she needed to think of a way to get it to him. She had a week, not more. It would mean bending a few rules, using some of her contacts. As the head of MI6, the much fabled 'C', that wasn't too much of a problem. But she would still need some help.

"Mike," she said, the two of them halfway through their Chinese takeaway dinner. "You still have plenty of contacts down in Hereford, don't you?" She glanced up at him, then took another forkful of food.

Mike looked up at his partner, a puzzled expression on his face. "You know that I do," he allowed.

"Contacts that could sort out some weaponry for me?" the lady continued. "Fast. And get it into to Italy."

"Legally or otherwise?"

"Otherwise."

It was almost ten o'clock now, the two men sitting in a shared car, as close as they dared to the villa. They were showing no lights, windows down, Alex watching the building through a pair of night vision glasses, a light intensifying device performing the same task at night as a pair of binos would do during the day. It was risky, recceing the target so soon, but this was the only night before the following Friday that they would get to see at first-hand what went on when The Pig and Shehu got together. It was invaluable.

"I know from the rumours that they eat first, abuse the women second. Normally they celebrate with a cognac or grappa afterwards. I expect that will happen on the balcony."

Alex nodded, hoping the same. So far they hadn't seen the two gangsters at all. If that remained the case, then Plan A was just about to be aborted.

"I could possibly get you a decent rifle locally," Gian continued.

"I'd need to fire it, to get it zeroed to suit me," the SAS man replied. "I can't see that working here. Rifle shots in the middle of the countryside would simply attract too much interest."

It was a good point, something that the Italian conceded immediately. The local police were fairly useless and corrupt, but gunshots would be reported. And the Sacra Corona Unita would also take a close interest in something like that. He nodded slowly. "You're right."

"And we'll only get one chance," Alex went on. "It has to be a weapon that I'm familiar with, one that is adjusted to my aim. The shot will be from about three hundred metres, so the scope has to be set up for me." He paused. "Janet will find a way." He handed the goggles to Gianluigi. "Your watch."

The Italian man trained the NVGs on the villa, watching and waiting for something to happen. The Englishman was right. They would only get one opportunity, then it would be time to disappear.

They appeared on the balcony at just after eleven, the two of them saluting one another with a tumbler of drink.

Even at this distance, the two looked like friends who'd just had a wonderful evening of fun, two cats that had got their cream. Dressed in loose fitting silk dressing gowns, they'd swaggered outside, drinks in hand. Alex wished that he had the means to take them both down right then, to end things tonight.

"Next week," he heard the Italian whisper. He glanced over, could see that his oppo was going through the same emotions as he was.

"Next week," he confirmed.

Special Delivery

The AS365N3 Dauphin 2 from 658 Squadron Army Air Corps lifted smoothly off the deck from the Credenhill military base, the home to 22 Special Air Squadron. It's mainly blue civilian livery reflected the early morning sun as downtown Hereford prepared for another day of work. At the controls Sergeant Peter Yardley and his crewman went through the usual checks, both ready for the long flight south. In the rear cabin sat a second aircrew, plus one long, cloth-wrapped item. Other than that, the aircraft only carried the munchies and drinks needed for the long journey.

"Two-One Charlie ready to exit camp boundaries," the young sergeant reported into his microphone. "Initially heading One-Eight-Zero, with an eventual transit over the capital and down towards Dover for the channel crossing."

"Roger, Two-One Charlie," the small control room replied, already having the aircraft's full flight plan. "You are clear to proceed."

Yardley pulled for more power on his collective lever, giving a push of the pedals to keep the aircraft straight, then edged the cyclic stick slightly forward, going into transitional lift, moving from the hover. It was something that he'd completed many thousands of times, a totally conditioned reflex. You didn't get selected to fly for the country's elite without being bloody good at your job.

In the back, the two spare crew members, adjusted the sleeping bags they'd chucked in, preparing to get their heads down for a few hours. Their turn would come. With a top speed of one hundred and eighty miles an hour, the journey would take over ten hours to complete. And then they had to bring the cab back home again.

"All this effort for a bloody sniper rifle," the crewman up front muttered.

"The pleasure of working for these boys," the pilot replied, thumbing to the camp behind them. "Never a dull moment with this crowd." He settled the aircraft into a steady climb, getting them up to an agreed cruising altitude of five thousand feet. It wasn't exciting, but it was going to be a great boost to his flying hours.

"First stop Brussels?" the crewman in the back asked over the intercom.

"That's right," the sergeant pilot agreed. "We'll grab a coffee there, have a bit of a comfort break."

"Time for a kip then."

The cabin descended into silence, the only interruption the pilot checking in with the various control towers along the way. The two reserve flyers in the back switched off their own intercoms, happy not to hear all of the chatter that kept the helicopter safe. It would be their turn at the controls soon enough.

The second stop was Milan's Malpensa Airport, right on the edge of the Dauphin's range limit. Another coffee, another pit stop, but also time for a crew change, the first two aviators now on the edge of their allowable hours for the day.

"From here to Rome, then the trip down to Brindisi. Find the drop off, then same route home with an overnight in Rome," the new aircraft captain unnecessarily informed the others.

"Sounds like an upmarket guided tour of Europe," the stood-down aviator joked, ready for his chance to get some sleep. It wasn't particularly tough flying, but it was boring, the only entertainment keeping the different flying zones aware of their presence. The rest of the routing had been sorted out by the Secret Intelligence Service. "If the stewardess could get the drinks trolley ready," he quipped as the rotors noisily ran up to flight idle. "I could murder a G & T".

They'd estimated that the aircraft would arrive at the rendezvous point at around seven that evening, light enough for the pilots to land without the need for NVGs, but late enough that most people would be at home. Inland from Brindisi, much of the land was given to agriculture, mainly vineyards and olive plantations, vast areas of planted crops that would make landing a helicopter hazardous.

"You know a spot for the bird to put down?" Alex asked. "There seem to be trees everywhere."

"This region produces forty percent of the country's olive oil," Gian replied, eyes on the road ahead. "About sixty million trees at last count. But yes, I have a spot for your people."

They were about fifteen miles outside of the port city now. It was just after six, so time to spare.

"I also have torches to guide the helicopter to us. It should be easy."

Alex nodded, comfortable that the Italian policeman had things under control. With the rifle in their grasp, they almost had all of the ingredients for the job. And still four days away from the next expected visit of the Albanian.

"How far now?" he asked.

"Ten, fifteen minutes," Gianluigi answered after glancing at the car's clock.

Alex pushed his skull back into the headrest, shut his eyes. "Wake me when we're five out," he said. It was a skill he'd learned from his early days in the military. Sleep when you can. You never knew when the next opportunity might present itself.

They were in the north of Puglia now according to the navigation system, eighteen minutes to run to their destination. Visibility was good, few hazards to be seen if you discounted the vegetation blurring by under them. Since crossing into the region the helicopter had dropped to only fifty feet, tree hopping across the landscape, avoiding radar detection, navigation lights off.

"Who are we meeting up with?" the pilot asked, the crew in the rear cabin now also awake.

"They weren't keen to say," the now rested senior aviator replied. "But unofficially, I heard through the grapevine that it's the Boss." Ranks were rarely used in the special forces, and the senior officer of 22 SAS was one of a few that had any sort of title at all.

"What the fuck would he be doing down here?"

The man in the back shrugged his shoulders. "I've been flying them for six years now," he said. "I've learned not to ask."

The two crew in the front glanced questioningly at each other, clear that they were not going to get more out of Yardley. The crewman looked in at the instruments, finishing his scan with another check on the computer map. "Five minutes," he told the rest.

"I'm still not seeing any holes in the foliage," the pilot replied. He began to slow the aircraft, looking for something down there that would indicate his landing zone. The others added their eyes to the search, trying to find a gap in the squat olive trees that covered the whole area.

A light appeared three hundred metres ahead, just a small beam standing out in the slowly descending darkness. "There," the co-pilot said pointing.

The helicopter was in a high hover now, about sixty feet above the ground.

A second torch beam appeared, both of them moving up and down, a symbol that the people on the ground wanted the machine to land in front of where they were.

The pilot checked the wind, found that he'd be landing head into it, confirming that the men on the ground knew what they were doing.

"Get the doors open. I'm going to land where he's indicating, but I want you all to keep an eye out for trees and obstructions. We don't need a blade strike out here."

The co-pilot swung his door open, locking it in place, the sound of the rotors drastically increasing as the rear doors also opened. "Our covert approach would be well fucked up if we buggered up our ride," he confirmed.

"Two persons down there," the pilot told them all. "Looks like we found the needle in the haystack."

The helicopter had been on Italian soil for all of two minutes, Alex entering the disk to collect his tool. He could tell by the look from the crew that they'd sort of expected him, but also that they hadn't believed that their information had turned out to be correct. It wasn't every day that you delivered an Accuracy International sniper rifle to the OC of the SAS in a field in Italy. One to tell the grandkids one day, he thought to himself.

They'd waited for a further five minutes to ensure that the aircraft had attracted no local interest, the rifle already stored on the floor in front of the back seat of the car.

"That went well," Gianluigi said softly. "Back to the city?"

Alex nodded. "Is there somewhere we can hide this for a couple of days?" he asked. "It's not the sort of thing that you want to keep in your hotel room."

The Italian stroked his chin, contemplating a good answer. It wouldn't be great for him to be discovered housing a sniper rifle in his lodgings either. It wasn't the weapon of choice for the gangsters of the SCU.

"I've found a boat," he finally offered. "Bought it with the money you passed to me. It's no good for serious sailing, but it will be fine for coastal stuff, or so I'm told." He shrugged. "You're the boat man, but maybe we should go and have a look at it."

"And store our supplies on it," Alex added, understanding the man's thinking. "Good plan, Gian."

"So what are we waiting for?"

Alex's experience with the Boat Troop had been mainly on RIBS – rigid inflatable boats with solid hulls – and Rigid Raiders, dancing around Poole Harbour, both of them small, fast, and highly manoeuvrable. What he saw in front of him now didn't fit any of those descriptions.

This was more like something that you'd see at a holiday resort as you hung onto a large yellow banana screaming for your life.

"What the fuck is that?" Alex stopped in his tracks, a look of horror on his face.

"It was just under five thousand Euro," the Italian objected, hands up in apology. "You said it was just for local stuff, close to the land. The owner said it would be fine."

Alex kicked himself for not getting involved in the purchase, even though he wouldn't have understood one word in the negotiations. At least he would have ended up with something that he considered half seaworthy. He shook himself – they had what they had. "My bad," he allowed. "It is just for coastal, plus the sea here is pretty flat from what I've seen." He grinned, trying to take the sting out of his initial comment. "Let's get on board."

He clambered onto the boat, guessing that the vessel was about five metres in length. The manufacturer was a Delta Marine, a brand he'd never heard of, the model a Corsica. The colour was a yellow closely suiting the giant banana he'd envisaged earlier. "How old is it?" he asked.

"The papers say it is 1979," Gian said. "Does it matter?"

It was dark now, hiding Alex's frown. They had a boat, but how long it would float was debatable. And if they had to get away in a hurry, there was no guessing that the engine would be up to it. "Not really," the SAS man lied. "We'll take it out tomorrow, see how she handles."

"I'm working."

Maybe for the best, Alex decided. He could take the boat out himself. No point getting them both killed.

"Let's get things stowed away and we'll call it a day." He was ready to call it a night, to run through the viability of his plans in the peace of his room. Maybe even to have a beer or two.

He spotted a long plastic storage box at the rear of the vessel that was secured with a padlock. He was about to ask how to get into it when Gianluigi passed him a key. "I don't get everything wrong," the man said smiling.

Alex shot him a return grin, trying to gauge the condition of the vessel in the near darkness, realising that he was simply wasting his time. It would still be there in the morning.

"You did fine," he allowed, but something in the back of his mind was telling him that he should have jumped into the Dauphin helicopter while he still had the chance.

Final Planning

In the morning the speedboat – if you could call it that – looked just as bad as it had the night before. As Alex climbed on board, it rocked from side-to-side, it's stability also questionable. An inspection of the hull would have been nice, but Alex didn't really have the equipment to do so. He leant over both sides, searching for cracks and holes, anything that might let the water in. Apart from the odd scratches where it had scraped along a jetty or twenty, all looked acceptable.

Alex opened the storage box, anxious to check the Accuracy International hiding inside of it. Here in the harbour wasn't the place to be doing that, even if the local police were the farce that Gian had advised they were. That would have to wait. At least everything was still there.

He found a floor panel that opened to reveal the engine, surprisingly clean looking and not particularly rusty. Maybe the owner hadn't cared about appearances, just about seaworthiness. It was a hope to hold on to.

Some seawater sloshed around in the motor compartment, probably the cause of the sluggish rolling motion. Maybe a bad thing, perhaps just rain. The boat could have stood for months in the harbour, something else he would have asked if he'd been present during the purchase. A faded plastic container floated in the water, and Alex lifted it out, began bailing out the mix of oil and other liquids.

He closed the hatch, checked through the keys that Gian had left him. It was time for the moment of truth. Would she start.

Initially the answer was no, but then he found an isolator switch used to protect the battery during long-term storage. He made the switch, tried again and the engine coughed into life, catching a few times before settling down to a steady purr.

"Seems that the last owner did care about his baby," Alex said to no-one. He had another look down into the engine compartment, checking to see that no oil or smoke was escaping from the machine. All good.

The SAS man was no professional sailor, but he was pretty sure in his mind that he had done all he could for the present. Now it was time to take the bull by the horns.

Slipping off the boats ties to the land, he pushed off the quayside, angling the vessel away from her berth. He memorised the number, hoping that it was his to use and would be there on his return, then pointed the Corsica towards the harbour entrance.

Five minutes later, he was in the quiet waters of the Adriatic.

After an hour of playing with the vessel, he was much more confident that she would do roughly what he had planned for her. He even considered taking her round the coast to get a view of the villa from the water, but that wasn't wise. Someone in that vast house would be watching for overly interested strangers, and anyway, it meant sailing around the headland, something he wasn't that happy to try just yet.

He took the boat further along the coast, spotting a small cove with a lonely couple sunbathing in it. He switched off the motor, dropped anchor, still a hundred metres from the shoreline, far enough for him to see the people, but not for them to see him. The boat took up the slack on the anchor rope, stopped and bobbled in the small swell.

"So let's have a look at what the boys have sent me," he mumbled.

Th weapon was well packed, a good sacking cloth outer cover, a waterproof inner, extra packaging around the important parts such as the sights. A sniper scope was wrapped separately within the same cover, twenty rounds of ammo in another waterproof bag. He checked serial numbers, pleased to confirm that both the weapon and sights had been the ones that he had completed his training on, both zeroed to his eyes. If he could reproduce under pressure what he had done on the ranges, he should be able to make a four inch grouping at five hundred metres.

Alex wasn't a sniper, but everyone in the SAS qualified on every weapon they could. When things went south there was no point making excuses, you simply just had to get on with it, whether the weapon was your favourite or not. Same with enemy weapons.

He slotted the sight on to the rails, clicked it into place on the top of the rifle.

"Sorry about this," he said to himself, placing the butt into his shoulder, his left hand gripping the stock. He raised the sight to his eye, placed his right hand next to the trigger mechanism.

"No bullets, so no panic," he muttered as if the couple on the beach could hear him.

Even with the slight rocking of the Corsica, he felt sure that he could get off a controlled shot. His grouping would go to hell, but that was fine. The weapon felt comfortable, undamaged in the transit to Puglia. And anyway, his planned shot wouldn't be taking place from a bobbing boat – that wasn't in his plan.

He lowered the rifle, setting it across a couple of cracked leather covered chairs.

"All looks good," he told himself and began stripping and cleaning the weapon, finally putting it back in its watertight cover.

Three days to go.

It was a risk, but one that Alex decided was a slender one.

They met in the city, not wishing to have both of them seen leaving it again. Though they met in different places, always leaving by car at the same sort of time might just get someone suspicious. So close to the operation, it just wasn't worth it.

Gianluigi chose the bar, a busy tourist one, somewhere that Alex wouldn't stand out too much. He was there when Alex arrived – just as they'd agreed – sat at the counter sipping a beer. The soldier had edged in next to him, asked his opinion on the local drinks. To anyone watching, it was just a bored tourist getting advice from a local. It happened all of the time, especially if the foreigner had no Italian language to his name.

The bar was busy, noisy. Talking without being eavesdropped on wasn't too hard.

"Everything works fine," Alex said softly once he'd finished making a play on getting his drink. "I tried out the boat, checked out the weapon. All good," he added.

Gian sipped his beer, looking disinterested. "What else do we need to do?' he said under his breath.

Alex shook his head. "Nothing." He checked his reflection in the mirro behind the barmaid, using it to see if there appeared to be any unwantec interest in the two of them. None. "We keep away from each other for the next day or two. Then on Friday I will be down at the docks again, make sure that our target arrives."

"I will be there to meet him. I can always send you a message."

The Englishman shook his head. "I like to see things for myself," he replied. "One of my old bosses often told me not to believe things if you hadn't seen them, touched them. I'll be there."

Gianluigi nodded, certain that it wasn't himself that Alex was questioning. He wanted to see things first-hand. If something was wrong, you could sometimes sense it, even if you couldn't put a finger on it. What they were about to do was massive – taking down the leader of the local Sacra Corona Unita *and* his main supplier from the Albanian Mafia was massive. The resulting shock waves if it came off would be like a tsunami.

"Okay," he allowed. "Any more thought on an escape plan?"

"I considered asking for the SAS helicopter again, but I'm sure Six would block it. They want no official UK involvement in this. If something went wrong, there'd be no hiding for them."

"So no plan?"

Alex considered the question. He did have ideas, but how to exit the area would depend on too many unknowns right now. And if he shared his plans and Gianluigi somehow got captured...

"Make your own plan. If we get split up, we both need an option. Keep yours to yourself." He stopped, feeling the mistrust radiating from the Italian. "It's for the best. This way, if all goes well, we have two choices of how to react."

The policeman nodded, the penny finally dropping. "I understand," he allowed. "And you're right. If one of us is caught, then we won't be keeping quiet for too long. These people are animals."

Alex drank the rest of his beer, shook hands with his oppo. "Thanks for the recommendation," he said a little louder. "Hopefully we meet again."

'Italy is a friendly place," the fake SCU gangster replied, also loud enough for the barmaid to hear. People here lived in fear of Sacra Corona, and eyes and ears were everywhere. "Enjoy the rest of your holiday."

Alex left the bar, window shopping, trying to spot the signs of a tail. Nothing.

He waited five more minutes, moving shop to shop, glancing occasionally towards the bar's entrance. He watched as Gian left, saw him carrying out his own counter surveillance practices, waited longer to see if he could see something that the Italian was missing.

So far they'd been lucky. Careful, yes, but lucky also.

No tail. At least none that he could pick out.

He walked back to his hotel, his mind whirring with the possibilities of how things might play out on Friday. Of what he would do with the rest of his life once his family was avenged.

He found no good answer.

Luan Shehu was well aware that Kola wanted him to stop the trips to Brindisi, that he was suspicious of what happened behind the closed doors of The Pig's palace. He knew that he should follow his head and not his heart, that now was the time to remove the pleasure trips from his weekly agenda.

His heart told him something else. Pleasure was pleasure.

"One final fling," he said to himself in the quiet of his office. "Then full focus on Kola's other operations." Who knows, he told himself. Perhaps he would find even more rewards on the other supply routes.

"One more."

There was little for Alex to do. The plan was complete, his exit strategy roughly mapped out, even if he had no exact long-term plan. Two days of nothing. Two days of looking like a tourist.

He visited museums, galleries, castles, and churches. He ate out in restaurants that featured in the tour guides.

If anyone was watching him, they would be seeing an Englishman on his holidays, someone who was attempting to immerse themselves in the local culture, escape the mundane boredom of the office job back home. A man at the end of his vacation, trying to cram in everything that he'd missed up until then.

He avoided the speedboat, simply passing the harbour during his wanderings to see that it was still there and attracting no interest.

He continued his counter surveillance routines, backtracking routes, using window reflections to covertly scan crowds, making abrupt halts to see if someone was tight on his tail. Though he knew he could be wrong, he was over ninety percent certain that no-one had clocked him or sussed him out as anything more than a British holidaymaker.

And that suited him down to the ground.

Sharp Shot

Alex had looked on as the speedboat from Albania arrived in the harbour at just after ten o'clock, observed the same people as the previous week leave the vessel. He'd watched as Gianluigi assisted two more girls onto the jetty, seen him carry holdall sized bags to the shore and put them into a waiting car. Nothing out of the ordinary if you were a pimp or a drug dealer, just a resupply from the proverbial corner store.

His target was right there, a simple shot from about seventy metres. So tempting. So impossible. He'd also spotted the muscle that the SCU had deployed to the pick-up, again the same as he'd expected. Wouldn't you put some security around the place if you had somewhere in the region of a million Euros worth of product coming ashore?

He wouldn't get out of the city. They'd chase him down, one man against too many. He'd get his man, but his time would be done.

Was that for the best? he wondered. He still hadn't managed to answer the question of what to do if this was a success. Africa? England? Heaven or Hell?

He dragged his attention from the activity on the quayside, lined his camera up on the view of the harbour. Once again, just a tourist.

For now, at least.

They met at just after seven at the boat, the sun already starting to drop towards the skyline to their west. The harbour was almost empty, the odd person still at their vessel, possibly preparing for a day hire, a fishing trip, maybe just completing a small repair. None showed any interest in the two men on the small Delta Marine boat.

"We need to get away soon," Alex instructed. "I'd like to get around the headland while we still have a little light left."

Gian climbed on board, dropping a plastic bag down on one of the spare seats. "Food and drink," he said seeing Alex's questioning look. "We need to drink, even if we don't eat the food." He settled into the forward seat next to the SAS man. "Ready?"

Despite the positive sound of the Italians words, Alex could sense the tenseness in the voice. That was good. What they were about to do would need focus. It was going to be dangerous.

"Ready," the SAS man echoed, keeping his thoughts to himself. He pressed the starter and the engine throbbed into life. "Let's go."

He slipped the last line, pushed the boat from the quay edge, prepared himself for the run out to the breakwater. He'd checked the weather, made sure that the swell was nothing exceptional, that the harbour authorities had issued no storm warnings. In the end, this was still a small vessel, and taking it out on open water in the dark wasn't the best idea he'd ever dreamt up.

"It'll get a bit choppier once we pass the breakwater," he told the Italian, suddenly realizing that he'd never been out on the Corsica. "But she handles quite well."

Gianluigi just nodded, watching the passing leisure craft, all of them dark and silent, home for the night. He looked back towards the quayside, checking that there was no new activity there, nothing to indicate that they may have been rumbled. He saw nothing.

They passed between the outer piers of the harbour wall, turned the vessel to the left and took a line towards the headland. All being well, they'd be down below the villa by eight, latest eight-thirty. Long before the two bastards inside of it had finished their fun, Alex thought bitterly.

But he couldn't help that. That would mean storming the place, and for a full frontal attack he'd need about twenty men. Ten minimum.

And he had two if you counted himself in.

The three of them sat for dinner, Il Porco deciding not to include the girls with the new man present. He could do that later, once the two of them had been working together for a while, once Shehu was out of the picture. It was a shame to change the business model, but sometimes there was no choice. He knew that embracing change was hard, that fighting it often seemed easier. But it was coming, so he had to take it on the chin. Shehu was going, being moved on. He would still have everything he had now, only with a new man to manipulate.

They finished eating just after nine, sipped a grappa at the table.

"I'm sorry I couldn't offer you a room, Fisnik" the Pig apologised as they drank. "Perhaps next time, when I have fewer other guests," he continued, sipping the fiery liquor. "But my driver will drop you at the hotel and collect you in the morning." He smiled pleasantly at the new man, not certain that he had the same tastes as Shehu. He knew that the man was married – family was all he'd talked about for the whole evening.

"No problem, and thanks for all of the hospitality." Fisnik made a sweeping gesture with his right arm, taking in the villa. "You have a beautiful place here. My wife would love it."

I bet she would. And maybe I'd love a turn with her, The Pig thought smothering the smile that almost escaped. "One day, you should bring her over," he offered.

"Thanks. I'd need to clear that with our boss, but it's a great idea. A holiday for her, a business trip for me."

Il Porco could think of nothing worse but nodded anyway. There was a knock at the lounge door, a suited man stepping into the room. "The car is ready," he announced.

"Perfect," the young Albanian said with a smile. "It's been a wonderful evening, but I'm tired out. A long day."

"I understand," the SCU leader replied. "We'll be off to bed as soon as you're gone," he continued, nodding towards Shehu. 'Only not to sleep', was the thought that ran through his mind. "As you said, another long day ahead."

They rounded the headland, the small boat rolling a bit in the swell, Alex keeping far away from the whitecaps, presuming that rocks lay somewhere beneath them. The sun was all but gone, the day now just a faint grey light.

Gian threw up over the starboard side of the vessel, sea sickness catching him out.

"Better out than in, as they say," Alex said, a wry smile on his lips. It faded almost as soon as it appeared, the SAS colonel realising that he hadn' cracked a grin in days. "You'll be fine," he conceded.

He steered the boat back towards the land, now clear of the rocky outcrop that made up the geology of the headland, the move lessening the effect of the swell. Gian took a bottle of still water from the bag that he'd brought on board, swishing his mouth out with it. He tried a grin, threw up again.

"Fifteen minutes," Alex said. "Fifteen minutes and we'll be there."

Gian sat back in his seat looking drained. "What about the way back?"

Alex stared straight ahead, concentrating on the route that he'd memorised from his laptop. He didn't want to look at his oppo. Didn't want to share the probable truth.

In his mind, he probably wasn't going back.

With Fisnik gone, the two men reverted to their usual animalistic ways, and rape was once again on the menu. Shehu was more bestial than usual, the knowledge that this might be his last trip sending him to new levels of depravity.

Once over, it was time for their time honoured practice of having a fine brandy or grappa and comparing notes.

"Your new man seems a bit of a goody two shoes to me," The Pig commented.

Shehu nodded his agreement. "I think that Kola pushed him my way. He wants someone on this operation that he has more control over." He shrugged. "I'll still be over occasionally, just not every week."

"The man is a bit of a control freak," the Italian agreed. "Something that I've picked up on over the years. He doesn't like his people having too much fun." He grinned at Shehu. "I'm sure he'd have a stroke if he could have seen you this evening."

Not for the first time the Albanian wondered if his host had anything on him. Hidden cameras, footage that might just emerge if things went wrong somewhere in the future. He'd seen nothing, knew that he was probably wrong, but it still made him a little nervous. If Kola knew he was taking a little on the side, then he was certain that his time on earth would be extremely limited.

'He always seems to give me space," he said.

"Be careful," Il Porco replied, his eyes flashing. "You've heard of the expression, 'enough rope to hang yourself?' I'd watch him."

But would you sell me out? the Albanian man wondered silently. It wasn't the sort of question he could ask, but it was always there. For the right money, he was pretty sure that the SCU man would drop him right in it.

"I'll watch him," he confirmed, not looking at the SCU leader.

"Let's go out on the balcony, enjoy the night air and a drink or two," Il Porco suggested, changing the subject. He'd made his point, let his supplier know that he had a handle on him, that he was the kingpin. That done, he was now ready to enjoy himself.

Alex knew that luck was with him, that he would have had no chance guiding the small boat to the wall of rock if conditions hadn't been so calm. With the weakening light, underwater hazards were all but invisible, but somehow they'd made it. Now they needed to find a way up the cliff, something that he'd half spied out during his earlier landside visit.

The light was fading quickly, the moon still on the up. They would be totally invisible to the men at the villa, too far away to upset the dogs.

"Here," he said, cutting the boat's engine.

A slanting fissure ran upward through the front of the cliff, just less than a metre in width. It angled upwards at about thirty degrees, enough space to let a man get into it and edge his way safely upwards.

Gianluigi looked at the fault line, understanding Alex's plan. "What do we need?" he asked.

Alex glanced around. "Somewhere to secure the boat," he offered. "Once we're done, this is the best way out. The other possibility would be the road, but that might be closed off by the security people up there. We should keep both options open though."

"Can you get the bow close to that crack? There's a small bush about two metres up. We could tie a line to that."

Alex nodded, picked up an oar, used it to push the vessel off a nearby rock, towards the opening in the rock face. It jammed in quite well, Gianluigi climbing into the gap in the cliff, bow rope in hand. He edged his way upwards, quickly reaching the foliage that he'd seen. He tied the painter to it, gave it a tug. "Okay," he called softly, confirming things were good.

"I think that this crack will get us all the way to the top," Alex said. "I'm hoping it also gives us a covered firing position, somewhere that we can see them, but they can't see us."

Gian stayed where he was, waiting for direction from the SAS man. "Shall I go up?" he asked when none came.

There wasn't room in the fissure for the two to pass one another. Alex would have preferred to lead, to be the first to get eyes on the target, but that meant the Italian coming down and getting back on board. At the end of the day, it didn't really matter. Whoever was first there had an equal chance of getting spotted, and then the game was likely up.

Alex grabbed the rifle, still in its waterproof cover, optics and ammunition also in the package. "Lead on Gian, but slowly. I'll be right behind you." He glanced at his watch. Quarter to ten, probably too early, but they could wait up there, get used to the lay of the land.

The Italian started climbing, edging slowly and silently towards the top of the cliff.

Luan Shehu didn't need to be told that they were drinking a good grappa. The yellow tinge to the spirit was a clear indication, but more than that was the warm glow it gave him when swallowed, not the burning, stinging, face twisting experience of the cheap stuff that he was more accustomed to. He swirled the little left in his glass, sniffed it, then tilted his head back and let it pour over his tongue.

"It's a good one," Il Porco said, a smile on his lips. "A shame that the women weren't of the same high standard." He held the glass under his nose, breathed in the fumes. "I guess they were okay," he allowed, then tipped the glass. "Another?"

"If you don't mind," the Albanian replied. "It might be a while before I get the chance again."

"You'll find a way, Luan." The Pig got to his feet, picking up the two empty goblets. "I'll be a couple of minutes," he said. "Enjoy the view." He pointed towards the dark water, the white moon reflecting off its smooth surface. "Great night for sailing."

"It is," Shehu agreed. "I'll come in with you," he added. "I have a small gift for all of your hospitality."

"There's really no need." The Italian frowned. "I'll miss our weekly get together," he said. "Likeminded people, same interests, and all of that. It's a shame it must end."

"Hopefully it's just a temporary glitch," the mafia man replied. "Come and see what I've brought."

Gianluigi reached the top of the funnel splitting the rock face, paused to catch his breath. No point in rushing to put his head out. Someone might be waiting, and he was in no race to die.

Alex stopped behind him, guessing that they must be at the top. "Can you see anything?"

"Just about to look. Thought I'd have a second first."

"No problem," the SAS man replied. "When you're ready. I need somewhere flat to unpack the rifle."

"They might not be there yet."

"I lay in a bush for six days once in Northern Ireland, just waiting to get a shot away," the soldier said. "Waiting an hour or two is nothing. Not if we can neutralise a couple of bastards." He checked himself, realising that he was getting anxious, the hate that had been there since the murder of his wife and kids breaking through to the surface. He needed this revenge, the sooner the better.

Gian looked down towards his partner, noting his remark as something out of character. He nodded to himself, pushing his concerns away. It was time to make an appearance, to see where this climb had brought them out. He moved forward, just allowing his eyes to get to ground level.

Nothing happened. No bullet, no dogs, no guards. No sign of anyone.

"It's clear," he allowed.

"Can I squeeze in?" Alex asked. It was tight, but he managed to wiggle his body past the Italian, the two of them now at the mouth of the fissure, heads just above the cliff, looking a little like two moles popping up in a garden. The thought actually made Alex smile, some of the tension ebbing away. They'd achieved phase one of his plan. "I'm going to get out of here, get behind that bush," he said, indicating a spiky plant less than two metres away. "I can set up the rifle there."

"Do you want me out too?"

"You can stay there if you're comfortable enough. Keep your eyes on the house, let me know if anything changes."

Alex placed his package on the ground in front of him, squirmed out of the hole. He focused on the villa for a full minute, searching for any sign that the enemy might know they were there, saw none. About three hundred and fifty metres ahead he could see the balcony doors from the building were wide open. He wasn't looking directly on to it, the fissure having brought them out to the right of the property, but it was still a very doable shot.

Not one that he would miss.

They stayed inside, the two of them sampling the Albanian raki that Shehu had brought as a gift, not nearly as smooth as the grappa, but something different all the same. Almost half of the bottle was already gone, the two men well on the way to drunk.

"We should switch back to the good stuff," Il Porco insisted. "You head out and I'll bring the glasses."

"It's a good idea," Shehu agreed. "A bit of fresh air might help us both."

He left the lounge, headed back out on to the balcony, dropping into his chair, staring out over the Adriatic. He closed his eyes, wished that Kola wasn't moving him on. This lifestyle was something that he wanted to maintain, and his boss was never going to allow that to happen.

The Accuracy International AX 308 was good to go, the sighting system locked in place, a ten round magazine in position. All Alex needed now was a target.

"Someone's moved on to the balcony," Gianluigi stated. He focussed the night vision goggles, concentrating on the distant image. "It's Shehu, the Albanian," he confirmed.

Alex felt his heart rate jump, forced himself to keep his breathing steady, to slow things back down. This was his time, this was his target. This was his revenge, the payback for what that man ahead of him had done to his family. His life.

He lifted the rifle, pulled the butt tight into his right shoulder.

"I'm not sure where Il Porco is," he heard Gian whisper. "Do you want to wait until they are both out there?"

Alex knew that it might be best, that the man would not come out if his partner in crime was dead on his balcony, that the sound of the shot would warn him of the danger. He should wait, get the two of them out into the open, take them both down. He steadied his breathing, placed the Albanian's head in the centre of the sight picture.

"What if The Pig has already gone to bed?" he asked.

His finger was on the trigger, taking up the first pressure, knowing a tiny squeeze would release the bullet that would kill his family's murderer.

"I'm not sure what's best," the Italian lawman replied. "You're right. It may be our only chance." He sounded uncertain, happy that Alex would rid the world of a drug runner and human trafficker, unhappy that the head of the local SCU might escape with his life.

Alex made the decision, drew another steady breath of air, started to release it slowly, squeezing gradually on the trigger.

The rifle barked into life, the round hammering down the barrel, charging towards the target that was less than four hundred metres distant.

Man Down

Luan Shehu was jolted out of his semi-drunken slumber as his seat toppled backwards and something large and solid landed on top of him. His head cracked on the tiled balcony floor, his eyes slamming open, his brain trying to sort out what the hell was happening. The mass on top of him was warm, and he quickly realised that it wasn't just a dead weight, it was a body. As he tried to move it off his own body, it dawned on him that it wasn't just a body, it was a dead one.

"Shit!" he swore to himself, desperately trying to free his legs.

A warm, wet feeling spread out underneath him, and a smell he was all too familiar with invaded his nose. The sticky wetness was blood, the smell death. He rolled away from the body, noticing that the dead man was his host, Il Porco. The man's eyes stared blankly at the sky, a look of surprise on his face. Shehu noticed a small patch of red high on his chest, the entry point of a high calibre bullet.

He didn't need to see the exit wound: that was where the masses of blood and internal body parts were coming from.

"Holy fuck!"

He was moving now, trying to get indoors. He had no idea where the shooter was, whether or not he was next up on the target list. There was only one place to get into cover, and that was in the house. From there he could assess the situation, get help.

He was fully free of the dead man now, crawling towards the doorway, keeping low. A bullet crashed into the doorframe, splintering the wood, making him stay down. Another round cracked over his head, hitting something inside of the building. He at least knew the attack was from the outside, that inside would give him a modicum of protection.

"Help!" he screamed. The Pig always had trusted troops within the house, far enough away from where the man completed his entertainment, but always there somewhere. He needed them now, even if their leader would never need them again.

"You took out Il Porco," Gian advised Alex. "He came out of the house just as you let the round go. He took the bullet."

Through the scope, Alex could already see that, could see that the Italian Sacra Corona Unita boss was no longer a danger to anyone in the living world, that the Albanian Mafia bastard that had killed his family had disappeared from his perch. One second. One second and his shot had been totally fucked up. His target was in the building now, unless one of his follow-up shots had got lucky. He didn't believe so.

"What do we do now?" the Italian policeman asked, his attention still firmly on the villa.

Before Alex could answer the question, security lights snapped on all around the building in front of him, the sound of dogs barking filling the previously still air. He could see movement through windows, more lights coming on inside. The security people were in motion, assessing the situation, making plans. Perhaps they'd let the dogs loose outside of the wall, and they'd certainly be calling for back-up.

"We need to get out of here," the SAS man replied. It wasn't what he wanted. He'd missed his intended target, taken out another animal, someone who had deserved to die, but his wife's killer was still out there. "Get back to the boat. I'll watch and slow things down if needed, then follow you."

He pulled the weapon back into the shoulder, moved his head until his right eye was tight on to the optics. A few shots into the rooms with the most activity, enough to slow up the guards a bit, another few to take out the closest LED lamps, cause more confusion.

His mission had failed, and now he needed to escape, to fight another day.

Luan Shehu had dodged death this evening, but that wasn't anywhere close to the end of it. Alex Green had a debt to draw in, and it was going to happen sooner rather than later. Right now, he just wasn't sure where or how.

He quickly packed away the sniper rifle, picking up anything that showed that the two men had ever been there, including the spent cases. A last look towards the villa, then he followed the Italian policeman down the crack in the cliff and back to the small boat, their only way out. The roads wouldn't be blocked yet, but others would be coming, and they couldn't get caught between the defenders and their incoming support.

Getting caught meant no chance of revenge, and that was never going to happen. Even if it was the very last thing that Alex Green ever did.

The SCU fighters had secured the compound, lit up the villa like an airport runway. Three carloads of reinforcements had been on the scene within fifteen minutes, bringing their numbers up to nineteen, every one of them armed. After establishing that no-one was within the grounds, they moved their search to the surrounding area, their leader indicating that the shots seemed to have come from the direction of the sea, either from a boat, or the cliff edge.

They released the dogs, let them do their work. Better a Doberman gets it than one of them.

The two animals barked a little, then started running around, searching the area, hunting down a target. It wasn't fast, the dogs not usually outside of the villa walls, the scents all new to them. Eventually one of them reached the top of the cliff, began barking excitedly. The second hound joined him, sniffing around by a bush, looking down the rocky crevice towards the sea. Though there was nothing left to prove it, the SCU men guessed that this must have been where the shots had originated from. The balcony stood before them, a tempting target.

More cars arrived, and by the morning senior Sacra Corona figures were on the ground. They had an operation to run, and that meant that they needed a new leader to run it.

Alex blasted the boat away from the cliff face, the water still crystal smooth, the moon glittering off its surface. He guessed that the guards would eventually release the dogs, that the animals would pick-up the scent, even if they had left no visible traces for the humans to see. He needed maximum distance between himself and the villa.

Gianluigi sat tensely, looking out over the bow. "Do you know the way? I can see nothing." He didn't sound too happy. Suicide wasn't something on his agenda, his wife's death happening years before, the memory not as sharp as Alex's.

"We have to move fast," Alex responded. "Once they secure the building, they'll let the Dobermans go. They'll find out where we were, guess that we must have come in by sea." He peered forward, searching for the headland, planning to take it wide. "We need to be in the harbour before they are. Otherwise we're done."

The Italian nodded, understanding that they needed to be off the water before the gunmen guessed their destination. "He'll go back home," he said softly. Alex knew who he meant. "That's where he'll feel safe."

"Right now, he probably doesn't realise that the bullet was meant for him," Alex replied. "But I agree – he'll be gone in the morning."

Gian was silent for a minute, his eyes still staring at the water, searching for danger. "What will you do now?" he asked quietly.

The SAS soldier let out a long breath, hardly aware that he'd been holding it. "Go after him," he finally allowed. "He still has to pay for his mistakes. He still owes me for murdering my family."

A silent nod from a man who fully understood the problem. "He'll be on his home soil," the Italian murmured. "There is even less law and order over there. And you'll be alone."

A bitter laugh, almost a bark. "I've been alone since he killed my family."

The ensuing silence was tense, neither of them knowing what to say to calm the situation, to make things better. They had achieved half of their objective, taken down the man who had led the local mafia, missed the man who had supplied that same persons women, drugs, and no doubt other contraband. On a personal level, Gian had got his payback. Alex had not.

"I could come to Albania with you," the Italian offered, glancing at the soldier. "Two is better than one."

Alex considered the option quickly, threw it out. "Your people have work for you here, and MI6 can't overrule that," he replied. "And I can't ask you to come with me on what is possibly a suicide mission," he finished.

The policeman took a few minutes to reply. "I agree with all of that, but I would still have come if you wished it. If not, how do we move forward?"

"Do you know which port Shehu operates from?"

"The Port of Vlora, almost directly across the sea from here. I think it must be about a hundred miles, but I'm not really sure. There is a ferry service, leaves from the port here daily." He turned towards Alex, finally taking his eyes from the water, ignoring the hazards that it might hide. "No way." He shook his head, swore softly in Italian. "Don't even think about it." Something inside him told him what the British man was considering. "If you're dead, then you never make him pay for what he has done to you. And a hundred miles of open water in this bloody thing..." He left the comment open, his accusation clear.

Alex ran his hand over a lightly stubbled chin. The man was right and had read his thoughts perfectly. Such a short time working together, but so much stress during that short period. Pressure drew people together, made them understand one another. And Gianluigi had totally understood his intentions.

"You're right," he finally conceded. "And I'd probably get picked up by their people immediately without Six organising some sort of legend for me." He needed another plan, but for now he simply needed to bring the two of them safely back to Brindisi port. "Let's focus on getting off this thing before the SCU suss us out. Then I'll talk to the office. This isn't over."

The Italian gave a sigh of relief. Whether he was a part of the future plans or not, there was no way he wanted to watch a good man throw his life away. Not on his watch.

"Take me home, captain," he said, forcing a tight smile. "We'll make a new plan, get the Bastardo," he added in his own tongue.

The little Corsica ploughed onwards, the headland dropping off to their starboard side. The harbour lay ahead, a few quayside lights now guiding them home. Alex's luck had held again. Now he needed to disappear for a few days, lay low. He could imagine that SCU activity in the town was just about to peak.

"Thanks Gian," he whispered.

Back at the villa, minds were clearing, people starting to think again.

"So we are pretty sure that they came in on the water?" Il Porco's deputy asked the on-site head of security. "Have we got anyone working the harbour, watching for unusual vessel activity? If they left from here, then they have to dock somewhere."

"I'll get someone around there now, but they could land a small vessel in any cove or bay, not use the port at all."

It was true but unlikely, the now most senior local SCU man decided. Docking in harbour at night was difficult, landing a vessel in a shallow bay in the dark needed a fairly skilled mariner or someone with good local knowledge.

"Get a helicopter up at first light," the man ordered. "Run it along the coast. Check for any abandoned vessels, anything that looks out of the ordinary. I want the people behind this."

Plan B

Janet had a dilemma; to bring Alex home, or to keep him on the trail of Luan Shehu. Home, he may or may not return to his position as the head of Britain's elite Regiment, the SAS. That would depend on a number of things, including his own willingness to go back to what had once been his second family. But it was also the same job that had caused the Albanian Mafia to go after his first family. Would he feel able to go back, to lead his troops, to take command once more, without personal feelings clouding his judgement? It was a major question that needed to be answered. A rogue soldier couldn't be allowed to run the country's elite force.

Leaving him to pursue the Albanian was option number two. That man had not only destroyed Alex's family but had also deliberately started a war on the British police force, taking down many of their number, leaving families without fathers and mothers, husbands and wives, daughters and sons. He was a person of interest not only to MI6, but also to their sister organisation, MI5. He was a viable – though not official – target.

But could she live with herself if she sent a soldier in alone, with no back up and no friendly assets in the country? Wasn't that just signing his death warrant? Was that her decision to make?

"You need to talk it through with Ruth," Mike advised her when the subject was discussed. Both of them were close to the Prime Minister – especially Janet – and Alex had got the PM out of trouble on more than one occasion with his actions abroad. "She needs to have a say in that choice."

Janet had spent plenty of time talking to Alex through Gian, knew how things had panned out in Italy. She was aware that the soldier still wanted to take down the Albanian, whether the government backed his decision or not. He needed closure, and the only way to get it in his eyes was to take down his family's killer.

In the end she decided to have a final call with him before taking the situation up with the Prime Minister.

"Would you not prefer to come back here, organise something properly?" she'd asked him. "It would still be off the record, but you would have all of the assets of Six and the Regiment to draw on."

"We don't know where the bastard even is, or what plans his organisation have for him now," Alex had countered. He was outside of Brindisi again, using his police colleague's secure connection. "Gian saw him leave for Albania but that's where the trail ends right now. A speedboat to Vlora, then nothing."

It was true, Janet knew. MI6 had no information coming from Tirana, no agents to call on in Albania.

"I will approach my Italian counterparts, see what they are hearing," she offered.

"Gianluigi is doing that anyway, but he has to be careful. The new man supplying goods to the Sacra Corona is unsurprisingly nervy, still unsure what the attack was all about. It looks like they believe it's some sort of turf war, someone trying to take their business." He paused, checked his surroundings, making sure that his Italian oppo was out of earshot. "I just hope that they don't start looking internally. I know that it has taken years to get a man inside of their circle, but if they ever suspected him..." He didn't need to finish.

Janet knew that she was batting on a losing wicket, that Alex was right. If they waited long enough, Shehu would disappear. He might be moved to the US, to Columbia, Afghanistan. It might take years to get another chance.

"Think it through carefully," she pleaded, hoping to keep both options open. "Let's talk in a couple of days, see if things have settled. The SCU still need a supplier, so perhaps Shehu will return, give us another opportunity."

"Two days," Alex had reluctantly agreed.

Which gave the MI6 leader forty-eight hours to convince the PM of the best way forward.

"I will not sanction sending Alex into Albania," Ruth declared at the end of Janet's short presentation. She looked tired, dark shadows under her eyes. The MI6 boss wondered when the PM had last had a full night's sleep, a proper rest. It made her feel even more guilty about the situation that she was now dumping on her.

"I'm not asking you to sanction it," she replied, pushing away the bad feelings. "It would be a deniable operation, something totally off the map. I just want your opinion."

"So now I'm just a sounding board!" the PM exclaimed. "Bloody hell, Janet, what do you want me to say?"

"I think she just wants you to know the situation as it stands," Mike interrupted, an attempt to calm things down a little. "We're talking about someone who is a friend of all of us. We are between a rock and a hard place right now, and neither of us two see a simple solution." He paused, hoping not to get blasted by the PM. They were close, but she was still the leader of the nation. Nothing came back, so he continued again. "If he goes alone, then he will probably not come back," he began.

"And we will lose one of the greatest soldier's our country has ever produced," Ruth retorted.

"He may already be lost to us," Janet said quietly. "What happened to his family will change him forever."

Ruth put her head in her hands, sighed and squeezed her eyes tightly closed. "I get it," she finally allowed. "I really do get it. But I still don't want to lose him."

"I've suggested that he comes home, plans the operation from here, takes the right resources with him, either from Hereford or from Vauxhall. It would still be an off the record op, but at least I could support him," Janet said, trying to ignore the PM's final remark but finding that she couldn't. "We don't want to lose him either, Ruth, but if we just block him, then he'll probably just go it alone anyway."

"I think he's made up his mind to go," Mike added. "It's all about how much we can assist him."

The PM stood, paced across to the window, appearing to be searching for inspiration from the outside world. Finding none, she turned back to face the room. "Could the Italian policeman he's been working with be of any help?"

"That would blow his cover within the Sacra Corona organisation, something that they've taken years to put in place. It wouldn't be fair to ask." Mike steepled his fingers, watching the PM. "We could ask for volunteers from the Regiment, even from the South African side. I'm sure his brother-in-law would be straight there, but I'm also fairly certain that Alex wouldn't agree with that."

"It's just putting more people in harm's way," Ruth said softly. "And you don't think that he will come home, give us a chance to talk him out of it?"

"I've put it to him, but so far he's not committing," Janet confirmed. "This bastard Shehu murdered his wife and kids, targeted and killed our police officers. Alex wants justice."

Ruth was shaking her head, her hands balled into fists. "Do whatever you feel is right," she finally replied. "I cannot condone sending a member of our armed forces into a country with the aim to kill foreign nationals, but I agree that it is probably the right thing to do. We cannot appear to be weak on terrorists, no matter who they are."

"I'll talk to him in the morning, try again to get him to launch the operation from here," Janet said, already guessing that her suggestion would be refused.

"And I'll sound out the Regiment boys. I'm sure there'll be plenty who want to help out their old boss."

"Keep me briefed," Ruth Maybank replied. "But let's keep this totally off the record."

Back in Brindisi, Alex was pulling out his hair. The hours were ticking by, his quarry having a full two days lead on him now, the trail growing colder with every passing hour. His chances of finding Shehu were disappearing fast.

From London he was getting the same old tosh – come home, make a plan with us, we'll help you fix things. Promises. He knew that people were concerned about him, understood the problems of launching an operation in a foreign country without the backing of the host nation. At the end of the day, London could promise everything, but in truth could give almost nothing. In the end, it would still be a deniable op, and he would be operating alone.

He lay in his bed, unable to sleep. It was a time for action, not words.

Enter The Lion's Den

As soon as Janet reached the office the next morning she organised things to have a secure call with Gianluigi, her only safe method for talking directly to Alex. On the way in she had been dreaming up solutions to persuade the SAS man to return home – Ruth Maybank had agreed to unofficially support her actions, but it was clear to the MI6 chief that the PM wanted her man back home.

In truth, so did she, and not just for herself and the PM. Mike Sanders had been Alex's boss for a long time, had grown highly attached to the soldier. And on top of all of those things, Alex Green had also been the muscle when Six needed it on too many occasions to remember. Still was.

She settled down at her desk, organising her thoughts, trying to work through the possible responses that might come back her way, then she pressed the button that held the Italian's secure number.

"Hello," a slightly nervous voice quickly answered. "Wait a second."

She heard a conversation in Italian between two men, sensed that the phone's microphone was half covered, distorting the words. A few seconds passed and she guessed that the undercover policeman was moving to a place where he could speak more freely.

"Hi, how can I help?"

"Are you alone?" Janet asked. Usually she sent warning of her calls, gave her people a chance to prepare. "Can you talk?"

"I'm at work," Gianluigi replied quietly. "But I can talk for a short time."

Janet understood. The man was 'at work' and this meant with the SCU, not the Italian police force. She needed to be careful and quick. "So Alex isn't with you?" she asked, answering her own question. "Can we organise that I speak with him, perhaps this evening?"

There was another silence at the end of the phone, and she could imagine the man looking around, checking for anyone within listening range. "I can't do that," he said, and again it sounded as if he was on the move.

"So he isn't with you?" she offered, hoping she would get a straight answer soon. She heard a ship's horn blasting from somewhere in the background, knew that the man was likely somewhere in Brindisi harbour. "But maybe tonight?" she tried once more.

"I'm afraid it's impossible," the Italian replied, the ambient noise suddenly all fading away. She heard a door close, imagined that the policeman had moved into an office, a shop or something.

"Why?"

"Alex left on this morning's ferry for Vlora. He should be there by now."

Janet felt her heart jump, the hairs on the back of her neck standing to attention. "Vlora?" she said stupidly.

"He said he couldn't wait anymore, that the trail would go cold. I offered to join him, but he said I was needed here. That I am the only one who can monitor things on this side of the water." Gianluigi stopped, waiting for the MI6 leader to respond. Nothing came, so he continued. "I told him that it was more dangerous over there than here, that the authorities there were even more corrupt. He ignored it all, went anyway. I tried talking him down, but..." His words ran out.

Janet's mind was finally operational again, trying to think of ways to salvage the situation. "So he may call you," she stated, realising that if Alex had no contacts in Albania, then the Italian might be his only way to find out where his target now was. "Is that what he said?"

"First he will try and find Shehu – find him, kill him. But he's a realist, knows that the man has several days head start on him. We also know that the Albanian has been replaced by a new man, so he must have a new job."

"So perhaps he doesn't even return to Brindisi, is that what you mean?"

"Perhaps, but then at least we have the replacement to go after. I have to maintain that link. It is our only back-up plan."

And not much of a one at that, Janet thought. She shut her eyes, trying to imagine what the SAS colonel might do next. "Listen carefully," she ordered. "If you can reach Alex, or if he reaches out to you, I need to know ASAP. I want to help him. I want to keep the man alive."

"And so do I," the Italian replied softly. "So do I."

The Red Star vessel poked it's bow between the breakwater walls at the Port of Vlora five and a quarter hours after it had left the protective shelter of Brindisi harbour. It had passed Sazan Island twenty minutes earlier. Alex knew from his research that the island had been used as a submarine base in the past by the Italian, German and Soviet navies, and that the port was the second largest in Albania. It had been a choppy crossing, and one that Alex now knew he would never have completed on board his small Corsica class speedboat, now languishing back in Italy.

The SAS man had slept for most of the crossing, finding a quiet corner and keeping a low profile. Sleep had been hard to come by after his attack on the Sacra Corona Unita villa, and the gangs activities had visibly increased since the loss of their leader. It was just a matter of time before someone discovered that their small yellow vessel had been missing from its moorings, that the times coincided with the attack, remembered that a foreigner had taken it out on daytime sailings over the previous week. He'd had no real choice but to move. Hanging on longer would have let Shehu get too much of a head start but would also have put both Gianluigi and himself in mortal danger.

He hoped that his Italian colleague was still safe. He'd intentionally not involved him with the preparation of the boat, only used him in the final purchase, though the funds had been transferred online using an account that Six had set-up. Nothing should be traceable back to Gian. The man might still prove to be his only way back into the Albanian gangs.

Alex felt a pang of guilt for not waiting to talk to Janet Anderson, to not holding on that extra day or so. Procrastination might be the killer of time, but it could also be the killer of people, often taking away the element of surprise, a weapon that he was going to need in spades to make this venture have any chance of success. Waiting not only made it more likely that he would be discovered, but it also allowed the Albanians time to make themselves more secure, to look into their shortcomings. He couldn't allow that.

He checked his passport, still running under the legend that MI6 had provided him for his entry to Italy, again just another tourist. Thousands passed through the border every day, and the SAS man decided that one more shouldn't raise any suspicions from the immigration officials. He considered stuffing a few Euros into the picture page, decided it could do more harm than good. If too many questions were asked, then he could resort to bribery as a last hope.

The ship was now drawing alongside, the dock workers gathering in teams to receive her lines, to secure her and allow the unloading process to begin.

Alex stood on the deck, looking out over a town that he'd never seen before, a country that he'd never visited. In that maze of streets he needed to find a weapon, shelter, somewhere to plan his next move. More than all of this, he needed to find Luan Shehu.

He checked into a cheap hotel, a bed, a shower, a breakfast in the morning, not exactly tourist accommodation. He paid in cash, had withdrawn the last of the funding he'd received from Six before he'd left Brindisi, a little over six thousand Euro. He'd converted it into Albanian Lek in a seedy looking currency exchange, a toothless old man giving him a rip-off rate of seventy-five Lek per Euro for the two hundred Euros that he'd converted. Everything about the place was shouting 'poor' at him, from the beggars in the streets, to the shifty looking pimps watching their women out of their first floor windows.

It was easy to see that the country was one of the poorest in Europe.

Before searching out his target, Alex needed a gun, probably a decent combat knife too, though any knife at all would suffice. If he was going to take the war to the mafia, he needed the tools of his trade.

He unpacked the few things that he had with him, wondering if he might have somehow got his snipers rifle through an incredibly lax border control checkpoint. It was now buried out at where the Dauphin helicopter had dropped it off less than a week previously, Gianluigi the only person in Italy who knew it's whereabouts.

Getting a knife would be easy, he decided. Getting a gun much harder, and liable to attract attention from others who would also have access to weapons. Buying one would be unwise, even from a backstreet trader. But there were other ways to get what he needed.

He lay back on his bed, shutting his eyes as he tried to visualise a working plan.

He had been alone on operations before now, had been in positions of no support, won through, but right now he felt more alone than ever in his life. Absolutely no back-up. No Regiment to call on when things went tits-up. Not even Janet to try and cover his arse.

It was a rude awakening, and the first time that he really felt that he'd made an error of judgement in chasing Shehu.

Dead, he was worth nothing. Dead, he couldn't avenge his family.

He shook off the bad thoughts, chased his demons deeper into his soul. He'd made it before, he'd do it again. It was good to feel anxious. Being blasé in a tight situation wasn't clever. It got you killed.

He sat up on the bed. It was time to get out there.

He chose the backstreets, the places that tourists wouldn't enter. He hoped that he would stay anonymous, that the people who worked in the rundown brothels and bars would be more interested in making a little money than remembering some bloke in jeans and a T-shirt, a baseball cap pulled low over his face.

The individuals who glanced his way looked rough, faces tanned and lined, the effects of hot sun and cold winters he guessed. They were the type of folk who lived hand-to-mouth, not the richer thugs that were a part of the mainstream mafia.

He could find them later.

The criminals here were the bottom feeders. The women would turn you a trick, the men sell you a packet of drugs, the action taking place in the dark corners of bars, the shadowy street corners, profit margins tight. They were the final links in the chains that had started far away in Afghanistan, Columbia, and the likes. The big boys at the top had made their money. Now it was all about what you could eke out down here on the streets.

Alex ordered a beer, sat at a street table outside of a bar, a wall at his back. He could watch from here, suss out who was who in the Albanian zoo. Somewhere here would be a controller, a pimp, a headman. And people like that would have their own protection. A weapon.

He wanted that weapon, whether it was a firearm or a knife. Preferably the former.

From there he could start his search, upgrade his equipment as he progressed. In a city like Vlora he was confident that there would be plenty of opportunities to get whatever he needed. And then he would be ready to take out Luan Shehu.

The target was moving carefully between the bars, stopping and having silent conversations with people as he went, a girl here, a dealer there. Money was exchanged, his cut in whatever service the person had been performing. You could watch it anywhere on the planet, whether it be London, Amsterdam, or Akrotiri. It was the dark underbelly of society, something that normal people were blissfully unaware of.

The man was about Alex's height – about six foot – and stocky with it. He wore jeans and denim shirt, his hair dark and lank, his front teeth both chipped, face scarred. He had the look of a bar bouncer, a school bully. For the SAS soldier, he'd be easy meat.

Alex was on to his third small beer, stretching them out while he decided on his plan of attack. He'd been propositioned twice by the bargirls, turned them both down, the others getting the message. He wasn't here for that sort of thing. He'd watched the man do his rounds twice now, seen him disappear back towards a building just off the small square. That was where his den would be, where he either had his home or a small office. Probably the former.

The man in the denim shirt was about halfway through his third collection, and it was time to move.

Alex signalled the barman, put some Leks on the table. Beer was cheap, but he didn't want to leave too much. That was also going to get him unwanted attention.

He walked purposely along the main route that led out of the area, getting out of sight of the bars, and then backtracking to where the denim shirt would leave the square on the way back to his HQ. He needed to get there ahead of the man, not to lose him in one of the dozens of small hovels that formed the main accommodation in the area. Once the man was back in that rabbit warren, he would lose him until his next cash circuit, if there was to be another one that night. Alex had no intention of repeating his night's work the following day. It was all about now.

From his new vantage point looking back into the square, he could see that Denim was leaning in close and talking to one of the ladies. He seemed to be annoyed with her, gesticulating at the woman, possibly because the girl hadn't brought him enough money for the evening. Alex watched as he took her roughly above the elbow, marching her forcefully towards where he now stood in a shadowy doorway. The girl struggled to free her arm, the man now getting a grip on the back of her neck, frogmarching her away from the safety of the drinking dens.

Alex doubted if anyone would intervene. It was likely a scene that the staff witnessed most nights of the week, but it was a problem for him. He didn't want witnesses to what he needed to do. With his target only paces away, he needed to make a decision, and fast. He stepped out of the doorway.

The man's eyes flashed in Alex's direction, obviously surprised at his sudden appearance, then he spouted off some angry words, a man used to being obeyed in this neighbourhood. With his free left hand, he moved to brush Alex aside, to continue on his way. He had a woman to punish, a business to run.

The SAS man allowed the push, rolled off the target, initially letting him pass, but only for a second. The Albanian didn't even look back, his dominance on this street complete, at least in his own mind.

He didn't see the soldier's foot rushing towards the back of his left knee, but certainly felt the connection, his leg effectively disappearing from beneath him, dropping his body down to the ground.

Alex knew that he needed to be fast, to take the man down and out before he could raise the alarm. He pushed the girl away from them, dropping down and smashing his knees into the small of the man's back, a move that would either break or bruise the man's ribs, or if the connection was lower, hammer into his kidneys. Either would do, but neither would keep the man quiet for long.

He leaned forward, grabbing for the man's neck, not going for the throat and the respiratory passages, but for the artery carrying life giving blood to the brain. Cut that off for even a short time and the man would be out of it.

Denim struggled, but he was winded from the fall, hurt from Alex's drop onto his prone body. For the soldier it was all too easy, a fight that was over before it had really got off the ground.

He felt the man go limp, scanned around him to see if he'd attracted any attention. He could always say that the girl had been in danger if needed, that the thug was threatening her, but he was pleased to see that no-one was to be seen. The girl sat on her haunches just a metre away, a look of shock on her face, unsure whether or not to run.

"Speak English?" he asked, knowing that he was giving away more than he liked. It was a chance that he would have to take. His eyes were on the woman, his hands swiftly searching her pimp. "English?" he tried again. Time was against him. He needed to move.

"A little," the woman whimpered. "He kill me for this." It was clear that she was terrified, even if the situation wasn't of her making.

"Where does he live?" Alex asked, finding no weapons on the man. Still no sign of any other interested parties, no twitching curtains at windows. The alleyway was fairly dark, a place that only residents might chance. "You know his flat?"

The girl nodded.

"Take me, now," Alex ordered. He'd found no weapons but had extracted a wad of cash from the man's front jean's pocket. It was a mix of drug and sex money, far more than the girl could make for herself in a month. "This is yours. It means you can get away from him." He hoped it would help, would add anything he found in the man's flat to the reward. "Show me his house."

Denim was still out for the count, a dead weight, so Alex just grabbed him by the legs, a sort of reverse wheelbarrow, dragging the body behind him. The girl gathered herself, got up.

"This way," she said pointing, indicating a nearby block. "Just over there."

At last some good news, the soldier thought to himself. He needed to get them all off the street, away from prying eyes.

He bundled the unconscious body through the door of the nearby apartment block, through a downstairs doorway that the girl had indicated and they were alone. The place was a tip, an unmade bed, a dirty kitcher area, a table, bundles of cash stacked on it. Alex grabbed a pile, handed it to the woman.

"Get out of here," he ordered. "Go away to your family, away from this bastard," he added, nodding at the man.

The girl looked at the bundle of notes, uncertain what to do. "He will kill me," she whispered.

"That's why you must go," Alex said. "Go to another town. Are you from Vlora?"

A shake of the head, her eyes still on the money.

"Then go to your home. Start again." He pressed the notes into her hand, finally getting some sort of response, the girl stuffing them inside of her bra. She glanced at the table, turned back to the door, uncertain. "Take more," Alex told her. He didn't need the money, just a weapon.

The woman grabbed another bundle, rushed out of the room before this madman changed his mind.

Alex pushed the door closed behind her. He needed to be out of there and fast. The prostitute might have a change of heart, alert others. He started a search, his focus the kitchen area and the counting table. This was where the man spent most of his time, and that meant he would have his protection close to hand.

Alex pushed back a chair from the table, and there it was. Not a pistol he would choose to use, but a gun all the same. Ancient, Russian, a Tokarev TT-33 handgun dating back to World War Two.

"Beggars can't be choosers," he muttered to himself.

He took a kitchen knife from the drying rack, a three inch blade that would have to do. A last look around, a glance out of the window, and then the SAS soldier was on his way, mission accomplished.

Finding The Target

Back in his hotel room, Alex locked the door and started stripping down his newfound toy. He disassembled every part of it, including the working parts and firing pin, noting the wear in the trigger mechanism. The weapon had rarely been cleaned, probably used more for show than shooting. He moved on to the magazine, finding only six rounds inside of the box casing, two less than full. It would have to do, better than nothing.

The weapon hadn't been oiled for years, rust evident on many parts and also visible when he scoped-out the barrel. Going out and buying gun oil and a cleaning kit was out of the question, so he'd need to improvise, possibly with some sort of metal scouring pad and some cooking oil. Anything was better than nothing, and he needed the old Russian military handgun to work if things got tough. A stoppage at the wrong time was likely to be the death of him.

He locked all of the parts in his bag, chucked the kitchen knife in there with them. It was time to go shopping.

"Do you have anything on the man?"

Gianluigi tilted his head back and sighed, hoping that the phone's speaker didn't pick up his despondency. Alex fighting his private war on the enemy's turf was not a good thing, and he could see just one outcome, and not a good one. "He's gone off radar," he eventually said. He needed to give the SAS man something positive, but nothing much came to mind. "He's been replaced by this new guy, Fisnik," he added, almost as an afterthought. "He's still operating out of Vlora."

"And they use the same launch as before for the journeys?" Alex asked, clutching at straws. Perhaps this Fisnik was his only link to Shehu.

"The same boat, the same sort of supply line, just a different man doing the same job," the Italian replied. "And a different man running the show at this end too." A slight grin spread over his face. At least something good had come out of this whole affair. Il Porco was no more.

"Just another criminal profiting from ruining other people's lives," Alex said bitterly. "Sorry, Gian," he continued. "I just want to get this thing over. Settle scores."

The Italian remained silent again, considering his next words. "And then what happens?" he asked.

Alex shrugged, the mobile phone hiding the gesture. "One step at a time," he finally offered.

The weapon was ready, the corrosion removed from the working parts, the barrel lightly oiled, the rounds cleaned up. It would never be perfect, but it was in far better shape than when he'd liberated it from the pimp. He'd have liked to fire off some of the bullets, to try and zero the pistol, but with only six chances he couldn't be throwing them away on niceties.

Now he needed to find a link to his final target, Luan Shehu. And that link appeared to be someone called Fisnik.

It was time to find the mafia gang's vessel, to get eyes-on the only man he knew who could guide him to his goal.

He tucked the Tokarev into the back of his jeans, pulled a lightweight jacket on over his T-shirt, hiding the weapon.

Vlora had a sizable harbour and he needed to swiftly find a needle in a haystack.

He left the hotel.

Fisnik now understood some of the reasons that Luan Shehu had enjoyed his old position, the company speedboat plodding along at low speed into the safety of Vlora Harbour. He felt like some kind of millionaire, his own private vessel running weekly trips between Italy and Albania, bringing him riches that he'd never dreamt of in his previous role. It was good for him, good for his family. His wife had never been happier.

As a family man he knew that what the mafia did was intrinsically wrong, but as an Albanian he knew that this was just a way of life that had been going on for decades. He felt a tiny twinge of guilt at the thought of the two girls he'd left with the new SCU warlord, knowing that their lives were about to change forever. He didn't give a thought for the drugs and the misery that they would eventually bring to someone. Drugs were a way of life, something that kept you going in stressful times. It was all about controlling your use of them.

The vessel nudged against the fenders on the quay wall, slotting silently into its berth, the journey over for another week.

A night at home, and then he would start preparing his supplies for the next run, whatever that might include. Drugs, people, weapons, alcohol – none of it mattered to the mafia man. This was simply work, work that meant more time and money for his family.

For him, that was the best of all worlds.

Lady Luck was obviously smiling down on him.

Alex had headed for the leisure part of the port estate, the place that the pleasure craft, both large and small, bobbed at their moorings. It made sense. A speedboat didn't belong in the commercial harbour, wasn't a ferry or cargo ship.

And there it was, right in front of him, drawing into a floating jetty, the captain cutting the engine, tossing a rope towards a man on the dock. The same vessel he'd seen Shehu arrive on in Brindisi, his cargo of illegal merchandise ready to be handed over to the buyers from the Sacra Corona Unita.

The boat's line was attached to a small bollard, a man leaping up to the quayside, turning briefly to salute the man at the controls. He was smiling, obviously pleased to be back home, a man happy in his work.

"I need to check that it's Fisnik," Alex told himself.

But he was almost certain. A crewman was assisting the captain to secure the launch, pulling weather covers into place, checking the security of knots. Meanwhile, the man who'd jumped ashore was heading towards the gate that would put him back on terra firma, a man on a mission.

Somehow, Alex needed to follow him, to find out where he lived. Then he could verify his identity.

And after that he could use him to find Shehu.

The taxi dropped him off in a quiet residential area on the edge of the city, not overly affluent, but quite nice for a 'working-class' region. Fisnik hoped that one day soon he could move somewhere more up-market, show his wife the full benefits of his new position.

He took his overnight bag from the back seat, paid the driver. It was good to be back home, but now that he'd seen some of the trappings of the new SCU chief he wanted to be a part of that set.

Okay, there were risks associated with the job, that was clear, but the rewards for his family far outweighed the dangers.

His front door flew open, one of his kids running down the path to greet him.

The taxi halting at the far end of the street was the last thing on his mind, his counter surveillance training out of the window.

"Bebe!" he called to his young son. "Bambino!" he added in his new local tongue. The boy was up to him now, Fisnik dipping down and taking him in his arms.

Fifty metres away, Alex noted the position of the house and paid his own cab driver with cash. It would be a long walk back to the hotel. As he left the car he added an extra hundred Lek to the fare, pulling his baseball cap lower over his face, trying to remain anonymous. Asking a taxi driver to 'follow that car' wasn't the best way to stay below the radar, but he didn't have the benefit of team to do the job inconspicuously. It was something that he had to live with.

He waited as the car pulled away, pretending to tie his shoe.

A close reconnaissance, basically just a walk by the target property, and then he'd withdraw to prepare his plans. They would be basic. 'Simple' meant less to go wrong.

He needed to know where to find Shehu.

Alex was a highly trained killer, but that didn't mean he was heartless. Killing Fisnik to get the information that he required was fine, but involving his family was not. The man had a wife and at least one child, that much he had seen, so he needed to think of a way to get the man alone. Interrogating him in his own home was a nonstarter, even though he knew that the man's mafia employer would think nothing of doing the same.

It meant that he needed to stakeout the house and wait for the man to leave its safety. And that needed a vehicle.

Hiring was out – it would need ID documents, a credit facility of some sort. Even with his fake papers, that would leave a trail leading back to him. That wasn't an acceptable option.

It meant he needed to steal a car, something that wouldn't be noticed as missing for a few days at least. And where better to get one than from than Vlora Airport. Choose someone who was obviously packed to be away for a little while, a family with suitcases and kids, a businessman with hold luggage. Of course it was risky, and his victim may just return the following day, but as a rule of thumb it would work.

Hotwiring a car was all part of a day's work, even the ones with electronic ignition systems. He'd attended lectures on how to manage these things, had practiced in Hereford, used the skill when required on operations. When you needed transport, then you needed transport. One way or another.

He researched bus times to the airport, set his plan in motion.

Fisnik left his home early, hoping to complete his work quickly and enjoy the afternoon with his family. He hopped on to his Vespa scooter – something that he hoped to change sometime soon, though it did have its advantages when the traffic was bad – and pointed it out of the estate. He had a few meetings to complete – suppliers and dealers – and also one with the senior Capo in the area, Kola. The thought of that one set his nerves jangling. It was also his first of the day. The man had a reputation for not suffering fools gladly.

He steered his way down to the main road, heading out of town to where the mafia leader lived. He failed to notice the stolen green Fiat that followed him out of his estate. It was seven in the morning, a time that many residents made their way out to earn a crust.

"A car would be so much better," he mumbled to himself. Especially for the meeting with the boss. His cheap Vespa would stand out like a sore thumb

"Perhaps he'll feel sorry for me," he continued with a grin, the wind blowing his words away.

Alex followed at a safe distance, considering whether he could somehow force the scooter off the road. With the morning traffic he would need a viable reason, something that wouldn't get other drivers involved.

He decided it was wiser to wait, to let things pan out for a while.

Holding his position about eighty metres back, he wondered where the mafia man was going, his route taking him out into the countryside outside of Vlora. Maybe to a supplier, either drugs or girls. It didn't matter.

He shifted in his seat, wishing that he'd 'borrowed' a larger car than the Fiat 500X. It might be good for young eighteen year olds that had just passed their driving tests, but it wasn't so great for an aging soldier who was six feet tall.

He looked around him, taking in the barren brown slopes dotted with clumps of bushes, the odd farmers field, olive trees. He had no doubts that the local crime gangs took money from every business around here, and he couldn't begin to guess how the people made ends meet. It certainly wasn't England.

His gaze switched back to the Vespa ahead of him, noticing that the traffic was thinning a little, wondered if an opportunity might present itself soon.

Fisnik spotted the driveway that would lead him up to Kola's residence, a modern building that had been designed to look like a small castle and turned off. Two minutes later and he was at the electronic gates of the place, pressing a button to speak to the main house.

The gates swung open, a voice telling him to proceed. He moved forward, the gates closing behind him, again wishing that he was here in a car. He'd never make Capo looking like this.

He drove fifty odd metres further on, arriving at a paved parking area in front of the three storey building, noting the black Range Rover and the rose red Lamborghini already stopped there. Did it mean that Kola already had guests, or were these just a part of his trappings?

"I really need a car," he again muttered to himself.

Alex pulled over to the side of the main road, watched as the Vespa paused at the gates, rode onwards. He was too far back to intervene, and anyway, the building at the top of the drive belonged to a rich man, and there was no doubt he'd have some sort of surveillance on the gates.

This wasn't the place to take action, at least not today.

He turned the car around, took up a position on the opposite side of the road, now facing back towards the city.

It was time to wait.

"How was Brindisi?" Kola asked once Fisnik had been escorted to his opulent office. The place was full of heavy wooden furniture – teak, if Fisnik wasn't wrong – a drinks tray in one corner, a long dark leather sofa and three matching chairs dotted around. "Take a seat," he added, gesturing to one of the seats.

"It was fine," Fisnik replied, continuing on with a breakdown of what he had traded and the prices obtained. He'd come prepared.

Kola nodded, pursing his lips in appreciation. "You did well," he said. "A drink?"

"I'd prefer not to, boss," the junior man replied, hoping that the title was acceptable. Maybe 'sir' would have been better with such a senior man. "I have more meetings in town after this."

"And I see that you are on two wheels."

Fisnik blushed, guessing that his approach had been monitored on CCTV. "It helps in town," he offered, again wishing that he had a proper vehicle. "Beats the traffic."

"I have my own bike in the garage," the gangland leader said, trying to settle the younger man. "But perhaps we need to find you a car. Looks better when you are dealing with the suppliers." He smiled.

Fisnik hoped that his embarrassment wasn't too obvious, tried to think of a decent answer. "I'll start looking," he offered.

"No need," Kola replied. "I'll sort things out for you." He stopped, rang a small brass bell. "Coffee?" he asked. "And then you must tell me more about the trip. How the Sacra Corona are faring after the loss of The Pig." He grinned, hoping that his own nickname wasn't so insulting. "And any other rumours that might be circulating over there, including any about the activities of our own people," he added staring deeply into the younger man's eyes.

Fisnik knew better than to ask for clarification. His boss was basically ordering him to deal the dirt on Luan Shehu.

Kola's reputation for seeing all was infamous.

It was going to be a long morning.

It was also a long morning for Alex, sitting in the car in the hot sun and waiting for his target to leave the mansion. 'Hurry up and wait' was as much a part of military life as was shooting a rifle. Long periods of inactivity, interspersed with brief moments of utter chaos. It was something that you just had to get used to, like it or not.

He took out his phone and sent a message to Gianluigi, just asking if he had anything new on Shehu. The reply was almost immediate and in the negative. Nothing new to report, only that the Italian had forgotten to tell him that Janet Anderson wanted him to get in touch with her. Alex considered the request, decided against contacting the MI6 lady. She would only attempt to lure him back to England, and right now he was not ready for that. Maybe once he'd evened the scores with Shehu he could consider re-joining Hereford, but now wasn't the time.

He settled back in his seat, watched the road.

Two and a half hours and a series of torturous questions about just what had happened in Brindisi on the night that Il Porco had been taken out. Kola had wanted every detail, which wasn't easy for Fisnik to provide, his own accounts all second and third hand. Shehu had been the only man present, and he had been very evasive about it all. The guards who were first on the scene could only recount what they'd discovered after the event, and they hadn't been too forthcoming about sharing that with the new man from across the water.

"So Shehu was actually there, but you were not?" Kola asked, clarifying what he already knew.

"Yes. The Pig wasn't expecting me, didn't know about the changes we had planned, said he only had a room spare for Luan. I was to stay in a hotel." Thank God, he thought to himself. One of the recurring questions from his boss was regarding the intimacy between the Italian SCU leader and his colleague, Shehu. It was as if that was some sort of a betrayal to the Albanian Mafia, as if the man had sold out to the enemy. He was again pleased to have been housed elsewhere.

Kola nodded. "And were there any rumours of what went on during these stays in the villa?"

Fisnik shifted uncomfortably. He had heard stories, was uncertain as to their authenticity. "Eating, drinking, talking," he said softly. He knew he had to continue or lose the trust of the headman. "Sex with the girls he was transporting," he added. "At least, that is the gossip amongst the Sacra Corona people." He stared at the floor, hoping that this was enough.

"Gossip?"

The junior man glanced up, looked into Kola's face, looked away again. "From several sources," he allowed. "Including the house staff. I think that it may be true."

Kola nodded. "Do you think he was also trading privately with the man?"

Not for the first time, Fisnik blushed, knowing that he'd already said more than enough. "Rumours again," he said. "But it would be easy enough to do. You give us all a lot of freedom." He hoped that this would placate his leader, end the session, and it did.

Kola stood, poured them both another coffee from the pot on the side.

"You will do well," he told Fisnik. "Don't get greedy and I will look after you. Keep your eyes open. Find out how the new SCU man operates. Don't cross the line like your colleague seems to have done." He sipped the lukewarm fluid, set down his cup, the meeting done.

Riding out of the electronic gate, the young Albanian wondered how his boss would handle the Shehu situation. At the end of the day, it wasn't his problem. His priority now was to get the next shipment together.

He reached the main road, turned back towards the city. His next meeting would be far less stressful.

And a car was in the offing. A real bonus. He couldn't wait to tell his wife.

Alex clocked the Vespa rolling down the hill towards the main road, started his engine. Traffic was sparser than earlier, but still a constant flow. He'd sit on the man's tail, see where things took him. He needed to find Shehu, but it didn't have to be that day. Rushing too much could get him into trouble.

They were heading back towards Vlora and the small bike would have advantages over the equally small Fiat in the city traffic. If an opportunity presented itself, he would strike.

He checked that the pistol was still in the door pocket just as he'd done about twenty times already that day. He knew where his target lived. He didn't need to panic.

Finding A Needle

The trucking company that Fisnik pulled up outside of was of course a great cover for both the drug and people smuggling operations that the owner was involved in. Both commodities needed moving from place to place, and there are plenty of spaces in a container lorry to hide things from the authorities, not that the regional police showed too much interest in the activities of the local mafia.

Alex considered his options.

The yard was on an old industrial estate in the suburbs of Vlora, other businesses close to hand, but none of them appearing to be doing too well. Some were boarded up, windows smashed, doors hanging off hinges, their trading days appearing to be over.

The SAS man had no idea how many people worked for the lorry firm, or whether he could take down his man on the premises. Without that information, this would be a risky option. Better to grab the mafia man alone.

Alex pulled a cheap black balaclava he'd bought from the car's glovebox, placed it on the passenger seat beside him. He knew that he must be getting soft, planning to quiz the man without killing him, not wanting to hurt his family. Shehu had caused the death of his own wife and kids, but Fisnik didn't look the type of man to be doing the same sort of thing. His decision was to grab the man, interrogate him for as long as it took to get what he needed, then to get out of the place. It meant that the Albanian couldn't see his face. The car could be ditched, another one stolen.

The property beside the transport company was another of the estate's failed businesses, it's windows painted over. It shared a street that led to both of the companies. It was the one way in, one way out. He somehow needed to get the Albanian into that deserted plot. If it meant hurting him a little, then so be it. He just didn't wish to kill him.

He drove back to the street's entrance. Forty metres behind him was the entrance to the failed enterprise, fifty beyond that, the gate that Fisnik would have to exit to regain the main road. He turned the car, waiting for the man on his Vespa.

The truck company owner would be supplying three woman for the Friday sailing, would deliver them to the port at seven that morning. Partial payment was made, a generous mark-up applied, and the price communicated by SMS to Sacra Corona Unita. Acknowledgement received. He would check bank accounts later, ensure that the SCU had physically delivered the payment to his account. Then that part of his cargo was ready.

Next stop would be similar, a quiet meeting nearer to the harbour. Same routine, check that what he was offering was still acceptable to his end customer, then verification of payments. Business was simple, supply and demand.

"I'll see you at the boat on Friday morning," he said as he moved towards the door of the transport office. "Please don't be late."

He moved outside, looked to where his small moped was waiting for him.

"It will soon be a car," he said to himself with a smile. One more meeting, and his daily business was done. The kids were at school, his wife waiting for him in an otherwise empty house.

Life was good.

A green Fiat moved slowly from the main road towards him, the driver obviously not familiar with the area, crawling past a deserted looking hydraulic spares factory, pausing to read the sign. He kick started his Vespa, flicked the stand fully up.

One more meeting and then it was home to his lady.

Alex didn't just feign interest in the long unused factory. He studied the doors and windows, noted a brick walled refuse area off to one side, a place where he'd be invisible from the neighbours and the road. He needed to execute his plan and get the young Albanian in there as quickly as possible. Speed was of the essence.

The scooter roared into life, sounding far more powerful than it actually was, no doubt the baffles on the exhaust removed long ago.

He stopped the car just before the entry to the hydraulics firm, watched as he Vespa moved through the gate to next door's yard. Just seconds to go, time to move. He picked up the Tokarev, pulled the balaclava over his head, moved the car another couple of metres forward.

The scooter was on the road now, maybe thirty metres away, the rider watching him, probably thinking about asking if he could help, not seeing inside of the vehicle due to the glare of the sun on the windshield. Alex had positioned himself well into the road, slightly across the centre line, a man searching for something in a place that he really didn't know well. It left enough space for the Vespa to pass but meant it would need to travel close to the Fiat. Fifteen metres and closing.

As Fisnik drew up to the car, Alex threw open the driver's door, catching the handlebars of the bike, causing it to turn towards the small car, engine momentarily revving, the Albanian man fighting to keep it upright.

The soldier was out of the car now, balaclava in place, pistol leading the way. He grabbed Fisnik by his arm, the man still in shock, pushed him towards the rubbish area. "Move!" he ordered, jabbing the gun into the Albanian's stomach.

The car and scooter still blocked the road, a problem if anyone drove by, but it was a risk that he needed to take. He pushed the pistol into the back of the man's head, breaking the skin, blood running through the Albanian's hair. He needed to be quick, to get as much information as possible in the shortest time, and that meant making the man fear for his life.

"Where do I find Shehu?" he demanded. "Luan Shehu. Where the fuck is he?" He shoved the younger man onto the ground behind the brick wall, hoping that his luck held. "Shehu. Talk to me. Now." He kicked the mafia man in the ribs, enough to hurt, not enough to break anything.

Fisnik wasn't a stupid man, knew when he was beaten, his own weapon foolishly left at home in the house. "Shehu isn't here anymore," he replied in broken English, breathing difficult, hand touching his injured skull.

"I know that," Alex spat back. "I asked you where he is." He pushed the gun against the Albanian's forehead. "You've got three seconds."

"I don't have that sort of information," Fisnik mumbled. "He has been reassigned, given other things to do. Sometimes he will be back to report to the boss, but I don't know when that might be."

Alex felt he could believe the frightened man, but that didn't help his cause. He kicked him in the solar plexus, winding him. "I need to know who to talk to. I need to find Shehu. How can I do that?" He glanced at the car and scooter, knowing that discovery had to be imminent. "Who did you visit this morning? Was that Shehu's place?"

Fisnik had managed to gain some sort of control over his breathing, felt like he was going to throw-up. "That was Kola, my boss. He is also the boss of Shehu." As soon as it was out, he knew that it was a bad idea. Kola was ruthless and selling him out wasn't a great plan.

"Does he know where to find Shehu?"

The Albanian gave a slight nod. He didn't have any choice. It was either that or get shot. "He is the regional boss-man," he said, now absolutely sure that he was going to die, either by this madman or by his own people. "He will know."

The SAS soldier looked around, considered the best course of action. He would get nothing more from Fisnik, that was certain. It was time to go.

He smashed the grip of the Tokarev forcefully against the top of the man's skull, hard enough to knock him out, not with enough aggression to break bone. The man went down like the electrics had been switched off in his brain, out for the count.

Alex Green moved to the car, pulling the scooter away from the driver's door and onto the sidewalk, drove away from the industrial estate.

He needed a new car fast, and a new place to stay. Somewhere that wouldn't be on any of the tourist listings. It wouldn't be long before the local crime gangs had a price on his head. And now they knew that he was English, hotels and guest houses would be their first port of call.

Fisnik was groggy, his head throbbing where the gun had smashed into it, his eyes not finding focus yet. He had scrapes on his elbows from coming off the bike after the collision with the green Fiat, a gash on the back of his skull where the gun barrel had been rammed into it, and bruises on his torso from the kicks he'd received.

He pushed himself to his knees, checked to see if he still had a phone, checked the time. He must have been out cold for an hour, maybe a little less. He shook his head, trying to clear his vision, stopped when it made him feel nauseous. He used the wall to help him find his feet, spotted his Vespa lying on the sidewalk. He wondered if he could safely ride it.

Tapping in his password, he selected the number for his boss. Admitting what had just happened would be painful, but letting the man find out by some other method would be far worse.

And Kola would know what to do. His boss was brutal, but he had his sources, would know how to find the English bastard that had taken down one of his team.

Alex dumped the car in a backstreet nearby the port, wiping the steering wheel and other surfaces to make himself less traceable. He was angry, showing himself out but not really gaining too much ground. He'd seen Kola's home, knew that it would be well protected, much the same as the home of Il Porco back in Brindisi. A full frontal assault would get him killed, a long shot with a sniper rifle wouldn't get him the answers he needed, even if he had one.

He needed help, and the only person he could think of to provide any was back in the UK. Janet Anderson could search out a name, give him more background. It wasn't what he wanted to do, but it was an option, and he didn't have many more available.

"Is that you Alex?" the lady's voice answered. "Did Gianluigi tell you that I wanted to talk?"

Alex sighed. "He did but let me bring you up to date first. I need some help."

Janet gave a harsh laugh. "I guessed that much. That's the only reason that you're calling. Same as always." She attempted to keep the tone light, a part of her considering just what her friend might have got himself into this time. "You talk. I'll listen."

Five minutes later and the salient points were out there. "So now I need somewhere to stay, somewhere that can't be easily found by the mafia."

"We'll find a way," the Six boss replied. "And let me get on to my people about this Kola character. I'll come back within an hour." She disconnected the call, as usual a lady who wasn't wasteful with words.

Alex placed his pistol on the bedside cabinet, locked his room door and lay back on the bed. Suddenly, he was dog tired.

One man against the Albanian Mafia. The odds weren't good. Not at all.

"Are you sure that he was English?" Kola asked a bruised and battered Fisnik, having instructed him to return to the villa straight away. "Could it have been someone masquerading as a foreigner, trying to throw us off the scent. You said that he wore a mask." He was mad, but he needed to get the facts straight.

"I'm sure he was English. And yes, a balaclava."

"And he knows where I live?"

Fisnik coloured up, deeply embarrassed. "He must have followed me here this morning," he replied, conservative with the truth. "He asked who you were, whether Luan Shehu lived in this place."

"He knows Shehu?" Kola asked, considering what that might mean. "You say he was looking for him?"

"He asked me where to find him. Several times."

An idea sparked in Kola's head, a thought that might just tell him who they were looking for. "Did he look like he might be a soldier? A military type?"

The young Albanian looked up, surprised. "He did," he allowed. "Now that I think about it, yes. He knew what he was doing, could have killed me if he wanted to."

Kola was nodding, his suspicions confirmed. "Shehu killed his family," he explained. "His name is Alex Green, and now we will have to kill him."

Fisnik's brain was still only half working, the blows to his head slowing his thinking. "But how will we find him?"

"I will get our people to check the local hotels immediately," the mafia leader replied. Another option crossed his mind, even better than having his foot soldiers running around all of Vlora's many hotels. "But let's make him find us," he said softly. "Let's bring Shehu to Vlora."

Limited Assistance

"We've bought a one bed flat through an Italian shell company. It should keep you below radar for a while anyway at least," Janet explained over the phone. "I'll send the details via Facebook and SMS, divided up between a few messages. It will be safe enough."

"I appreciate your help," Alex replied, knowing he'd have been lost without it. Buying or renting something himself would have been a sure way of letting the locals know where he was. "Did you get anything on this Kola bloke?"

"He's a senior figure in the organisation, the main man in the region, running a number of operations in that part of Albania." She was careful not to say the name of the organisation. Alex would know that. "He also runs the supply operation across to Italy, so he is probably the man who reassigned your target."

"Was he also involved in the UK operation?" the soldier asked. That would make him a target too.

"Not certain yet, but he would have been your man's boss, so possibly. Don't forget that the man was dragged out of England at short notice after Andile's accident, so perhaps he just went a step too far and was withdrawn because of that. It's still work in progress."

Alex frowned, considering that option. He needed to find Shehu, and Kola was the clear link to get him there. "If you get anything more, please let me know," he requested.

It was Janet's turn to hesitate. "What will you do next?" she finally asked.

"I'm really not sure," the SAS man responded. "The boss-man will have protection, and I'm alone. But he seems to be the only route to my target."

"I could get you support from The Regiment, or even from my people," Janet said. "But it would be a hundred percent deniable. I can't have people operating over there legally without both their government and ours approving it."

Having people around him that he could trust was tempting, but an unsupported operation was just too dangerous to involve others. "Thanks but just leave it with me right now. Someone will slip up, give me the break that I need. It just takes time."

"Keep in touch Alex."

"It seems that you've stirred up a bit of a hornets nest," Kola said over the phone to his employee by way of introduction. "I want you in Vlora tomorrow."

"A hornets nest?" Luan Shehu responded, a little confused, but recognizing the caller's number. He wondered if the new Sacra Corona Unita leader had said something about his past activities in Brindisi, alerted Kola to the side-lines that he had been running. He felt a twist in his stomach, an uneasy feeling in his brain. "Can I ask what you mean?"

"You were moved from Britain in a bit of a rush," the senior mafia figure replied. "It seems that it didn't quite break all of your ties there. Someone came after you. He's now here in Vlora."

The fact that this wasn't about Brindisi didn't lower the tension that Shehu was feeling, actually increasing it slightly. "Alex Green?" he asked, his voice very quiet. Had the SAS colonel really come to Albania to take him on? Another thought surfaced – had Green been the man who had taken down Il Porco? He decided not to vocalise his thoughts, not yet. He might need a joker sometime soon, and this might be it.

"That is what I believe," Kola replied. "He interrogated Fisnik earlier today. Knocked him off his scooter."

Shehu suddenly realised that he felt very uncomfortable about going back to Vlora, and not just because of Alex Green. His own people seemed to be questioning his loyalty, and that wasn't a good position to be in. The problem was, if he didn't go, those same people would hunt him down, and the result would be terminal. Running was death. Staying, possibly the same.

"I'll be there tomorrow morning," he replied firmly, trying to sound positive. "I will sort out this problem. Green will die."

Kola grinned to himself, the answer one that he could live with. "Good, Luan," he said, his tone friendly. He failed to mention that he would also use the unplanned trip to discuss his junior's extracurricular activities over in Brindisi. First he needed a rogue British soldier off his patch.

A single bed, a small cooking area, a toilet and shower partitioned off from the only room that the 'apartment' had. In London it might just have made the grade 'bedsit', but that was fine by Alex. It was somewhere that he was totally anonymous, and far better than the thousand hedges, roof rafters, and rocky caves that he'd spent time in on surveillance during his military service. At least he had a toilet, didn't need to bag his own waste.

News on Kola had been less helpful.

The man was fairly much an unknown to MI6, but the Italians and Greeks did at least have a file on him, the man doing business with both, largely drugs and girls. 'Dangerous' was how the Greek authorities had labelled him, the Italians 'ruthless'. Neither were very complimentary – the man exploited people, made their lives a misery. They also said that he had a large local following, most connected through family ties, extremely loyal to the man. The local police were in his pocket, so seeking help from the law was a no-go.

"Is there some way to get a weapon to me?" Alex had asked hopefully. "Explosives if at all possible."

Janet's sigh told him the answer even before she spoke. "I can't help Alex," the Six chief replied. "I told you that from the outset. This is a totally deniable operation."

"Does Ruth know about it?"

Another frustrated groan, more information that Janet hadn't wanted to release. "She is aware of the outline details. She cannot know more," the lady said. "She's not happy but understands how we have reached this point. She would like you to come home, just the same as me."

Alex said nothing. Anything he could say would be negative, so he simply bit his tongue.

"What will you do?" Janet asked, fairly sure that the operation was about to be brought to an end, the odds against success just too large.

"I'll take down Shehu," the SAS man finally answered. "Right now, I'm not certain how, but that is exactly what I am going to do." He rubbed his eyes, trying to think of a way to progress the situation. "Thanks, Janet," he said after a minute. "I really do understand the mess I'm making, but you also can understand why I'm doing it. This is for Andile and the kids."

Janet grunted, her hopes that Alex might give up now gone. "Think about the offer for some back-up, legal or otherwise," she offered. "Take a day or two. Don't rush into anything."

Alex nodded at the phone, pressed the red button to end the call. He had nothing more to say.

He needed to find Luan Shehu, and the only person he knew on the planet who could possibly help him was some nutcase called Basri Kola that he knew almost nothing about. It wasn't a lot to work with.

"But I do know where he lives," he reminded himself. It was the only place left to try. He needed a break.

Finding A Break

Every nation has its own 'special' forces, whether they were a part of the army or not, but in Alex's eyes, the Special Air Service were still the elite. Like every good sports team, training and repetition made them perfect, and planning for the unexpected gave them the cutting edge. It didn't matter if you were the best golfer in the world, or the toughest rugby player, you had to hone your skills to make everything about your game second nature, and then you needed to have a Plan B for when Plan A failed. And in combat Plan A usually failed, often Plans B and C too. You needed to look at every possible scenario.

To even get started on a plan, Alex needed more information.

He knew that Fisnik was cannon fodder to the local mafia, that he wouldn't be informed about the bigger picture. Yes, he knew of Luan Shehu, but he had no idea of where the man now was or what he was doing. He could pump the man all day and learn nothing more than he already did.

Basri Kola was clearly the head honcho, probably not of the whole Albanian crime world, but at least of the regional gangs. He knew where Shehu could be found. He also knew by now that his operation was being targeted. That meant he would step-up his defences.

By now, he was almost certainly aware that Alex was English, and that he was interested in the whereabouts of Luan Shehu. Would he warn the man off? Would he not even inform him, just solve the problem himself?

And if Shehu was informed that an Englishman was hunting for him, would he run or fight? Alex was pretty sure that he would guess who his pursuer was. It wasn't rocket science. You destroy a man's family and he will undoubtedly come looking for revenge.

His choices were slim. He needed to talk with Kola, get him to give up his wayward lieutenant.

And that meant learning much more than he presently did about the man. About his home, his security, ways in and out of the man's residence.

It was time once more to go into surveillance mode.

And for that he would need more equipment.

Alex had studied the maps, found a road that ran about a mile above the rear of the property, on the opposite side to where he had watched Fisnik enter for his meeting. It was lightly wooded up there, allowing him a place to park his newly stolen car away from the road, out of sight of the casual observer. It wasn't perfect, but it would serve its purpose, and if found, then he would simply find another means of transport.

The woods were sparse but provided him with enough cover to descend towards Kola's house undetected, large pines somehow finding enough moisture to survive on the slope. From his elevated vantage point he could see over the property's wall, see into a large part of the grounds.

Alex removed a cheap pair of binoculars from his small pack, not the military standard items that he would usually have had at his disposal, but good enough to let him inspect the building from about a hundred metres. He'd bought them with the pack as a part of his surveillance shopping trip, both cheap in a backstreet supermarket near to his flat.

To one side of the building was an outdoor pool, not massive, possibly twenty metres in length. The opposite side provided parking space for the workers, probably for the security team, kitchen staff, cleaning people. Built off the rear wall was a lean-to building, the sloping roof making it look a bit like a conservatory back home, only with too few windows. A kitchen perhaps, or accommodation for the security detail? He would need to find out. It could be a possible point of entry.

He wished that he also had views on to the front of the building, allowing him to see who visited the mafia warlord and when. A regular visitor might be another route to gain entry, though they might have their own views on that subject.

The outer walls were approximately six feet tall, not difficult to overcome. He couldn't see any sign of CCTV or alarms around the grounds, but he remembered that the front gate had been operated remotely, meaning someone needed to monitor it. Cameras could be so small nowadays. He had to assume that his entry would be monitored, even if he managed to cut off the building's power supply.

Alex noted any points of interest, made a rough sketch of what was in front of him, plotting in windows and doors, possible entries and exits, to study back in his flat.

And then he made himself comfortable and settled in for a long wait.

He'd been in place for just over two hours, had watched armed guards leave through the back door of the lean-to building, usually doing their rounds with a small snack or a cup of coffee in hand. He guessed that the building was some sort of kitchen, and possibly situated next to the security personnel's quarters. So far he had counted four different people, and the patrols were on an approximate thirty minute rota. Weapons were MP5 machine pistols, something that Alex was more than familiar with. A real positive if he could capture one.

Traffic was quiet, only the man Fisnik arriving on his Vespa, scratched along one side following his meeting with the SAS man. He'd stayed just over half an hour, left in a small blue Alfa Romeo. 'A reward for his work?' Alex wondered. Sometimes getting beaten up by the bad guys could be a good thing.

He checked his surroundings once again, making certain that Kola didn't extend his patrols outside of the property, and ran another scan of the place through his binos. Nothing new. He considered stripping and cleaning his pistol once more, decided not to bother. If he got lucky, it would need to work just once, and then he would have a weapon of choice.

He ducked low, took a drink from a plastic water bottle, careful not to let it reflect the sunlight.

Alex raised himself at the sound of another vehicle crunching into the compound, watched as a Nissan SUV pulled into one of the gravel parking slots at the side of the house. He raised his binoculars, studied the vehicle, waiting to see who the new visitor might be.

A large man exited the car, a baseball hat pulled low on his forehead, pulling the shirt away from his back, obviously sticky with sweat after his journey. He stretched his arms heavenward, stood on tiptoes, shaking off the drive.

A guard moved from the lean-to door, MP5 slung across his back, sharing a joke with the new arrival. The new man removed his hat, returned a comment.

The bald head, the fleshy neck, the bulky figure. Alex couldn't believe his luck. Luan Shehu was right there in Vlora, not a hundred metres away from him.

He'd found his target.

Basri Kola allowed Luan Shehu ten minutes to get his overnight bag into the visitor's room, giving his lieutenant a little more time to consider his fate, then had a man bring him down to the front garden. He greeted Shehu, noting that the man appeared to be getting larger, his jowls sagging.

"Thanks for coming at such short notice," he said, offering his hand.

"It's no problem, boss," the man replied, accepting the handshake and man-hug, very aware that the two men were exposed and out in the open. The Pig had been killed by a sniper's bullet. Why would his enemy do anything different?

"We need to put this matter to bed, Luan," the mafia leader told him, getting straight to the point. "I cannot let someone roam around town taking down my people." He stopped at that, his message clear. Weakness attracted competition, and his rivals would happily capitalise on it.

"I understand."

"Let's walk and talk."

Kola linked arms with his visitor, guided him away from the house, turning midway down to the mansions walls. "What do we know about this Green character?" he asked lightly, guiding Shehu towards the swimming pool area. "What are his weaknesses?"

Shehu gave a swift briefing on what he knew of the SAS colonel, things that he'd learned during his time in the UK, well aware that many of the man's exploits would never be made public, hidden away in the cellars of Whitehall. "He was the man heading the operation against us in the UK. That's why I took out his family. I hoped that he'd back off," he finished.

"And it seems that he is doing quite the opposite," Kola retorted.

They were now past the pool area, moving towards the rear of property, the garden longer here. Shehu glanced towards the kitchen area, spotted a guard in the doorway, the man chomping his way through a bowl of olives, watching the two of them.

"He will make a mistake," he offered.

Kola grinned. "Let's hope so, for both our sakes," he said. "He made one in Brindisi, I believe, and look what happened there. The Pig died, you survived."

Shehu felt his guts knot, wondered how much his boss actually knew, where the conversation was heading. His eyes scanned the distant treeline, searching for threats that might be out there. "I will find him," he promised.

"Or he will find you," the headman replied with a smile.

Two men came into view, one of them his mark, the other probably the main mafia man in the area. He had seen no images of Kola, but the way he seemed to be leading the parade signified that he was the boss.

And it was a parade, a demonstration of power, but also a showing of the prize. Of course the man had to be guessing, but he was guessing right – Alex Green was doing what any soldier would do, reconnoitring his target, shaping his plan, deciding on how best to execute it.

Alex wished he still had the Accuracy International sniper rifle. A shot of just over a hundred metres with a scope would be unmissable.

Instead he had a Tokarev, an antique handgun.

He needed to think outside of the box.

They moved across the back of the house, came around to the parking area, the circuit just about complete. If someone was out there, they would have seen their goal. If not, Kola had at least reminded his lieutenant of just who the boss was.

"How will we find him, Luan?" he asked.

The junior man's eyes had been fixed on the slope above the house, searching the woods for anything out of the ordinary. He'd expected to hear the bark of a gun, a flash from a sniper sight, something that would indicate that the English soldier was watching, but he had seen nothing. Why would he? This was a Special Air Service officer, not some infantry grunt. Even angry and pissed off, this man would be damned good.

"If it is him, then he will find me," he finally said, knowing it to be true.

Kola smiled, not a friendly gesture. "That was my thinking too."

Alex had the outlines of a plan, but the odds of it working were incredibly long. If he was a betting man, then it was the sort of gamble that he would leave well alone.

He'd left his observation post as dusk set in, made his way back through the woods to the stolen vehicle. During the time there he'd definitely counted four guards conducting the patrols, with a possible fifth man he'd seen once watching from the lean-to doorway, then Kola and Shehu. Maybe seven members of the local mafia, men who doubtless had a reasonable command of their weapons. It wasn't an encouraging picture.

Back in Brindisi, he still had a sniper rifle and a small boat. He considered it as an option, knew from the ferry crossing that it was likely to fail. He crossed it off his list.

His only hope was speed and surprise, and the creation of a decent diversionary distraction. A pound of plastic explosive would be near the top of his shopping list, an airstrike would take out all of the risks, just a clear-up operation afterwards to check for survivors. Neither were within his means.

He turned on his two-ring gas hob, placed a pan of pasta on the burner. He was hungry but didn't want to show himself more than was necessary on the streets. No doubt his details were now circulated amongst the local crime syndicates, a price placed on his head. It was time to lay low, use only small shops for the minimal goods that he required to survive, his shopping choices avoiding the need for conversation. Speaking would likely betray his location.

He stared into the small pan, watched the bubbles forming at its base, the water heating.

Something sparked in his mind, a tiny light of an idea.

Gas. Could gas be the answer? The diversion, or perhaps the main tool?

He checked his hand drawn plans of the target area, began plotting how to make his attack work. The odds were still long, but a glimmer of hope was appearing.

He needed to sharpen up his plan, find a way to make household items into weapons of war.

Bitter/Sweet Revenge

Kola upped the security detail that night, their number increased from four to eight. If Green was going to attack, then that would be his choice of timing. Under cover of darkness, he could get up close and personal, silently take out his target.

His eight man team was based at the rear of the villa, close by the kitchen so that they could take care of themselves without entering the main building. The night-time patrols each consisted of two armed men, their frequency doubled, a team circling the property every fifteen minutes or so, the men working in four shifts to allow them all sufficient rest.

Kola and Shehu occupied two of the second floor bedrooms, another hurdle for any would-be attacker. The mafia leader felt that he had set the trap well, the bait difficult to get to without first disabling the eight armed killers on the lower floor, and then still having to find and take out Shehu and himself.

For one man operating alone, that should be impossible. Even for two, three, the odds were far against them. He felt safe, and he could decide later what to do with his wayward lieutenant.

He placed his 9mm Walther pistol on the bedside cabinet, stripped down to a pair of shorts, and prepared to go to sleep.

Three-thirty in the morning, a time when most humans on the planet were in their deepest sleep, at their most relaxed. Even those awake were not totally focussed, thinking ahead to the break of the day, knowing that their shift was nearly done, that home and a comfortable bed was soon to be theirs.

Alex parked in the same place as he'd done the previous morning on the track above the house, took his backpack out of the boot of the car. Inside were the tools he had assembled during a final shopping trip. Now he needed to set the trap.

He made his way downwards through the darkened trees, back to the site of his OP. Below him the house slept, a security light burning to the rear above the lean-to, one to the front silhouetting the property. A two man patrol started its circuit from the rear door, the two men talking quietly as they did their work. Boredom was setting in, the repetitive loop around the house no longer of any interest, dawn just about an hour off.

The men disappeared from sight, and Alex slipped from his cover and moved quickly to the property's rear wall, his pistol in hand. He lowered himself down to a sitting position, back to the wall, set the pack down next to him, opening it, the Tokarev resting on the ground beside him. He heard the chatter of the two guards returning to the back of the house, smelt the cigarettes that they were smoking, a clear sign that they were semi-professionals at the best. A glowing cigarette is a point to aim at.

He had a maximum of thirty minutes before the next patrol, possibly less during the hours of darkness. He would work on the latter, hope for the former.

A red plastic container came out of the backpack, Alex unscrewing the black sealing cap, checking the contents were still secure. A nod to himself, the cap back in place.

Tracking around the outer wall, he stopped close to where he estimated the swimming pool would be, looking for some dried out bushes that he'd spotted during his daylight surveillance.

Finding them, he placed the can in their centre, the top again removed.

Next out of the bergen came a packet of firecrackers, the sort of thing that kids would play with in the street, scaring dogs, cats, and old age pensioners. He attached them to a length of heavy washing line. He'd tested its burn rate in the flat, found that a metre would smoulder along with a small blue flame in about four minutes. He'd pre-cut a length of four metres, trailed it out away from the bushes, propping it up with small rocks to assist the flame. It wasn't perfect, but he hoped that his improvisation would work.

Diversion number one set.

He heard the sound of voices, checked his watch. He'd been right, the patrols increased during the hours of darkness. Not perfect, but not a surprise either. Fifteen minute intervals. He waited patiently, heard the men disappear, reappear about two minutes later, their rushed lap of the villa complete.

He lit the cord, hurried along the base of the six foot wall. He was on a timer now, had to get into position swiftly.

Again he estimated his position, threw the pack over the wall, then leapt as high as he could up the obstacle, pulling himself over the brickwork. He took a second to get his bearings, making sure no-one was in sight, then moved swiftly away from the barrier and towards the parked cars.

Checking his watch, he could see that he had ten minutes before the bushes should ignite.

Diversion two was cruder.

He picked the oldest vehicle in the parking lot, felt around for the petrol cap. As he'd hoped, no locking device, nothing to overcome. He unscrewed the cap, checked his watch once more.

Five minutes until the fun started.

"Time for another lap of the garden, then the next lucky boys can have their fun," one of the two duty guards stated, indicating the end of their shift. "Let's go."

His oppo extracted himself from his chair, cancelling the game he was playing on his mobile phone, some car chase thing that his son had put him on to. "Last one," he chimed in.

They left the kitchen, the keener man asking, "Left or right?" He'd asked the same question each time they'd headed out, anything to break up the boredom even by a tiny bit. His mate indicated right, and they headed towards the parked cars.

A low decibel whoomph came from somewhere behind them, stopping both in their tracks. "What was that?"

The answer was soon clear, a bright blaze starting somewhere just beyond the building's security wall. "So let's make it left this time," the bored gangster quipped.

They both rushed towards the flames, unsure whether they should get involved. They were there to guard the chief, not to put out fires.

"We'd better have a look before we call it in," the keener man decided for them both. Waking the head honcho up at four in the morning wasn't going to please him. Especially if it all came to nothing.

They continued towards the fire, its source still hidden from sight.

Alex dropped a handful of firecrackers into the open fuel tank, hoping that one of them at least would ignite the petrol fumes. It was a trick that didn't always work, and usually he would use something with a lot more of a bang. He moved away, seeking cover in some foliage, getting a good view of the hurrying guards and also the back door of the building. His guess was that everyone would be rushing out through it within a minute, and then he'd have a better idea of the odds against him.

The petrol tank suddenly blew, noisier than the last ignition, the flames reaching skywards. He watched as the two security men turned from their present objective, confused now about which way to run. They decided to split up, one continuing to the wall, the other turning back towards the cars. It was just as Alex had hoped. He waited, pistol in hand. There could be no half measures now – it was kill or be killed, so the man was going to get it.

And with any luck, Alex was going to get his hands on a Heckler & Koch MP5.

"What the fuck is going on?" the man said slightly breathlessly to himself. From nothing happening at all to a fire and an explosion in the space of two minutes had definitely shaken him up. "And where the fuck are the others?" he wondered.

Out of nowhere a man appeared, gun in hand. He saw the muzzle flashes, stopped in his tracks, ducking instinctively, but never fast enough to dodge a bullet in flight. It hit him square in the chest, throwing him backwards, arms spread, weapon falling to the ground next to him. He tried to retrieve it, aware that it was his only hope of survival.

A second bullet hit him in the stomach, the attacker closer now. He knew before the third round hit him that he was a goner.

The weapon wasn't adjusted to suit him, but Alex just aimed for the largest area of body mass, knowing that any hit would incapacitate the man until he was close enough to land the coup de grace. At five metres it was almost impossible not to hit something.

He fired his third round standing above the target, a bullet to the forehead and the fight was over.

He scooped up the MP5, quickly checked the dead man's pockets, finding two spare magazines. No time to check if they were full or not, just time to get back into some sort of cover and watch the chaos unfold.

The other guards were now pouring out of the rear of the building, half asleep and trying to make some sense of what they were seeing. One of their own lay dead or injured outside of the kitchen's door, a fire raged from the carpark, a smaller blaze still showing above the distant boundary wall.

The senior man barked orders, reminding them to make their weapons ready, shaking them into life, sending two men towards fire beyond the wall, two towards the cars. He moved with the final mafia guard towards their fallen colleague, ordering him to watch out for threats while he checked for signs of life.

He could see no sign of an attacker, but obviously the three incidents must have happened more or less simultaneously. That meant at least three hostile agents, more than the one they had been warned to look out for.

The man on the deck had a hole in the centre of his forehead. There was nothing he could do to help him.

He searched again for the enemy, wondering whether the next bullet would be for him.

Kola and Shehu arrived at the top of the stairs together, looked at one another for answers and found none.

"Alex Green!" the senior man yelled.

They pounded down the staircase, out of the front door. A second car was now alight, parked directly next to the first one, the tyres closest to it burning from the heat. The interior may well catch next, possibly the fuel tank. Better to avoid it, the two of them decided.

They moved towards the fence, found three of their troops there, one looking over the wall, shouting something about a bush being on fire. Shehu moved closer, Kola scanning the grounds of his home. He spotted the two men close to the house, shouted an order to bring them over. There was safety in numbers he reasoned.

Alex pulled the kitchen knife that he'd taken from the pimp in denim what seemed like a year ago from his bag. He heard the shout from the direction of the wall, thought that he'd been spotted, then saw the two men nearest the house start towards his first diversion. He looked over, could make out the bulbous shape of Shehu, guessed that Kola was probably with him.

That meant five men over by the wall, two still returning from the out of control car fire. Was that everyone? He was fairly certain it must be. If the boss was out there, then the rest of the team must be. Their careers would be over if they weren't.

Time to go.

He broke cover, sprinted towards the back door of the villa, hoping to reach it unobserved. He had things to do.

Luan Shehu saw something out of the corner of his eye, didn't know quite what it was, but a sixth sense told him that it had to be the enemy. It had to be the SAS soldier, the thorn in his side since his time in London.

"Someone just went through the back door of the house!" he called out, trying to attract Kola's attention.

"One of our people?" the mafia leader quizzed him.

"I'm not a hundred percent, but I don't think so." His gut feeling told him that it wasn't, but he didn't want to say that. "Maybe it's nothing. I just thought I glimpsed something."

Kola glanced at the dying flames that still smouldered outside of his property. "Come on," he yelled to his men. "We need to be in the house, not chasing ghosts." He looked back towards the front door. Out here he was exposed. Inside they could defend themselves much better. Shehu was probably just nervous, which was understandable. He was the target.

The team of mafia men moved back towards the front of the house.

It was a simple kitchen, somewhere that the hired help could fix a simple meal, grab a coffee. A couple of worktops, a microwave, a gas hob with a couple of pots on top of it.

Alex moved towards the last item after his swift evaluation of the place. He had limited time, needed to work fast. He'd been lucky: the place could have been off the grid, could have had an electric cooker. He pushed the thought from his mind, got on with the job in hand. It was only a matter of time before the enemy came back to the building, taking up defensive positions.

He turned on each of the four burners on the hob, smashed off the electric button that produced the sparks to light them with the butt of the MP5.

The smell of gas was quick, unpleasant, hissing out its presence.

He closed the outer door, moved over to the exit that led to the rest of the building, pulled that closed too.

The action was paused, giving Alex a few seconds to consider his situation.

This was drastic, but he thought that he could handle it. If the mafia troops came from the front, he could flee through the rear door, and if they entered from the rear, he could run through the house. He tried not to imagine what would happen if they attacked from both sides. At present, he still had the element of surprise – no-one was aware that he was in the villa.

He used the downtime to check the Heckler & Koch, quickly removing the magazine and pressing down on the visible bullet. It moved downwards only a few millimetres, telling him that he had a full load. He pulled back the working parts, ensuring that he had a round in the chamber, then clicked the mag back into place.

He was as ready as he could be.

Kola hung back as his team entered the reception area of his home, the senior security guard leading the way, weapon at the ready. They had seen nobody, but none were stupid enough to believe that no-one could be there. The carnage outside of the house hadn't happened by accident.

"Check upstairs," the mafia boss ordered. It was natural to feel safer when defending a position from a height. He wanted his team to be up there and ready to defend any further attack. At least until daybreak dawned.

"He might be up there, so be careful," Shehu advised. If he'd been correct, the man had entered through the back door, but that didn't mean that he was still there. He too would want the advantage of height.

"Two of you check the back of the house," Kola commanded.

Two men approached the kitchen area, checking rooms as they moved towards it.

The smell of gas was horribly strong now, and Alex knew that he had to do something soon or get out of the building. He could hear voices at the main doorway, wondered if more people would come to the rear. He could hear nothing out there, but it would be a great ambush – drive him out the back door and have a team waiting to mow him down.

He needed to do something, something to drag the mafia crew into the scullery.

He opened the back door, the fresh air outside pouring in. He sucked it in, felt his senses sharpen. Outside he could see nobody. It was time to take a chance, to try and rush the enemy onwards.

He slammed the door as loudly as he could, stood just outside of the house, listening for the advancing mafia crew.

The two men heard the slamming door, looking back to see if the rest of the team had also picked up on it. They had, all now advancing towards the kitchen area, caution fading. Their quarry was on the move.

"He's escaping!" Shehu yelled. "Quickly!"

All nine mafia men stormed towards the closed kitchen doorway, anxious to catch the man who had already caused so much destruction.

The first man slammed into the wooden door, pushing it open ahead of him. He immediately smelt the sickly smell of gas, tried to back off, only to be pushed through the entranceway by the arrival of the other men, and then they were all moving into the kitchen.

"Gas!" the first mafia man shouted in warning.

Alex heard the inner door crash open, booted open the back door, careful to keep to one side, letting off a burst from his machinegun, catching the first man just above his waist. He counted four men, could see that there were more behind them. Another swift burst of about five rounds, screams and shouts punctuating the air. He needed a spark, something to ignite the noxious fumes of the gas before it dissipated from the two open exits from the room.

He ducked out of the doorway, seeing that the men were recovering from the shock attack, weapons coming to bear on him.

Shehu clambered over two fallen bodies, trying to get to where his enemy had disappeared. His pistol was raised, pointing at the kitchen door. Alex Green was out there, the man who had caused him so much trouble. It was time to end it, time to end him.

Alex swung back into the doorway, weapon at the ready, fired another burst, his aim not at the men but at the gas hob. One round bouncing off the hob's metal frame would produce the spark that he needed, the one that he hoped would blow the kitchen to pieces.

He spotted the bald Shehu charging through the room, pistol at the ready, dropped to the ground, rolling away from the man's aim.

The Albanian reacted on reflex, his target in his sights, his hatred for the man brimming over, his nemesis right there in front of him.

He fired three rounds in quick succession.

He heard the shots crackling past somewhere above his body, his luck holding out once again. He kept on rolling, making himself a hard target.

Alex had seen the results of gas explosions on the television, whole houses going up and looking like something out of a war zone, every floor of buildings destroyed, neighbouring houses often the same. He hoped to get a fraction of that result, knowing that normally it took hours for a house to fill with the deadly fumes, that he'd only had ten minutes or so.

He didn't get what he'd expected.

The explosion was vast, taking out the whole of the back of the villa, knocking the wall down that separated the kitchen from the guards quarters.

Shehu took the brunt of it, his body taking flight and smashing into the rear wall, dead before he hit the floor, his clothes on fire.

Kola wasn't so lucky, his right leg snapping just below the hip after his body had been catapulted into the cooker top. His femoral artery was severed during the fracture, but he somehow kept his consciousness. It would take him ten minutes to bleed out, then he too would join his lieutenant wherever it was that dead mafia leaders went to.

Four more men died almost instantly from their wounds – they'd been directly behind Shehu, the man nearest to the epicentre of the blast. Two lay unconscious but still alive. The last mafia thug was lucky, had been at the rear of the charge. Apart from a gash to his right cheek, he was totally fine.

Alex was still desperately rolling away from the door when the room exploded. The roar deafened him, the flash from the doorway temporarily blinding him. He kept rolling, knowing that he had to get away from the building, guessing that the escaping gas would keep burning, possibly creating a fireball.

A shower of brickwork landed on his back, at first only a few pieces of masonry, then much more. Something big hit him as the lean-to roof collapsed onto his body, the rear wall also falling his way, smothering him in bricks and dust.

The SAS man tried to push off the debris that was swiftly drowning him, felt the impact as even more fell on him, cutting off his air supply, crushing his bones. He knew that he was losing the battle.

Images of Andile and the kids flashed through his brain, pictures of fallen colleagues, of victories and pain. Good memories, bad memories, things he'd forgotten had ever happened. For a second he thought that he might make it, cheat death once again.

And then the lights went out.

Afterglow

"What happened in Albania?" the PM asked, coming straight to the point.

Janet Anderson grimaced, knowing that her answer wasn't going to please her oldest friend. "To be totally honest, we still don't really know," she offered. "As you're aware, we don't have our own sources down there, rely on intel from the Italians and Greeks more than anything." She stopped herself, hoping that this might be sufficient for Ruth Maybank.

"Alex," the PM stormed. "What do we know about Alex," she ordered.

Janet steepled her fingers, trying to find the best words to give an honest answer. "We don't," she said, deciding that short and succinct was her best approach.

"We must have something."

Janet took a long breath of air, pursed her lips. "The Italians have confirmed that Basri Kola's residence was completely destroyed. They have been told that it was a gas explosion, possibly a fault somewhere in the system. The man was in residence, so he is believed to be one of the victims, but the place was totally devastated. They are still digging it out now, trying to locate victims."

"And was it all an accident, or was it the work of our man?"

"That we don't know Ruth. Alex had gone silent, non-communicative. After we organised the apartment, he never called back."

"So we have no clue as to what the Albanians might find in the wreckage of the building?"

"Correct."

"But perhaps they will discover a British soldier, a SAS colonel to boot!" Ruth Maybank was angry, not so much about the UK involvement, more about the loss of someone that she'd regarded as a friend.

"Perhaps," Janet allowed, careful not to make things worse.

"And Shehu? Was Shehu a part of this?"

Janet sighed. "We think so, but again this is another unknown. The Greeks tell us that he was visiting Kola, information from their local source. The Italians too. Nothing will be certain until the house is made safe."

Ruth Maybank silently assembled the facts and rumours in her mind. She wanted Alex Green back, wanted him to continue leading the Special Air Service, helping her to do her duty to the country.

"Let's say that the rumours are true, that Shehu was there in the villa, summoned for whatever reason by his boss, Kola. Let's say that the explosion wasn't an accident, that somehow Alex engineered all of it. Could he still be alive?"

Janet dropped her gaze from the Prime Minister's face, raised them again and noted the beginnings of tears in her friend's eyes. The PM had guessed the probable truth. "Ruth," she said solemnly. "Anything is possible, but we should prepare ourselves for the worst. Anything else is a bonus."

The PM nodded. "If he is alive, he would have been in contact by now," she whispered. "We have likely lost the best soldier the British Army has ever had."

Janet said nothing, the words already out there.

Ruth wiped her eyes with the back of her hand, picked up her glass of red wine, raised it, prompting the MI6 boss to do the same. "Alex Green," she toasted, her voice brittle.

"Alex Green," Janet returned the salute, a teardrop trickling down her own right cheek.

It was the end of an era.

Far away, in a walled garden just outside of Vlora, Albania, the authorities had finally proclaimed the site safe enough for the emergency services to enter the wreckage of a once vast villa. Walls had needed pulling down or stabilizing with wooden props, mechanical diggers needing to stand-off at a safe distance to complete the work.

Even before this, the gas supplies had needed isolating, something that should have been fairly straight forward, but no-one in the local council seemed to have any details on the services to the property. The rumour was, there were no records – it appeared that the villa's owner hadn't been paying for either gas or electricity forever.

Beyond the gates of the property, men in suits and dark glasses watched on, keen to be on hand when anything was uncovered. It was said that they had come from Tirana. Bulges in their jackets suggested that they were armed. Negotiations with the mayor would soon get them entry to the site. Under the pile of rubble they expected to find a number of their own people, maybe others. Something had caused this devastation. They needed to know what. Or whom.

A shout came up from the first group of searchers, a man with a long listening probe that was already half buried amongst the collapsed brickwork. Others moved towards him, their excitement visible even from the villa's entrance.

"There's someone alive in there!" the cry went up.

Watching the scene from a spot slightly elevated from the site, Gianluigi held his breath. He didn't know it, but his choice of surveillance point was very similar to the one his colleague had used only days before.

He took out his phone, considered calling London, decided it was probably too soon.

He had no idea how many people had been in the property when the explosion had demolished it. Maybe someone was still alive in there, but that didn't mean it was the man that he'd been sent to search for.

No point getting people excited yet. False alarms didn't help anyone.

He took a sip of water, checked again on the progress below, watching a large excavator move forward slowly to assist the searchers.

Anything was possible.

Thanks for reading this latest novel. I hope that it went down well and that you have time to review or rate the book using your local Amazon site. You can find links to this and more of my stories at –

https://amazon.com/author/gordonclark

Special thanks to the Defence Imagery Website where I found the original photograph for the book's cover, using it under the terms of the Open Government License. The photo has been filtered and sized to create the final cover image.

"Contains public sector information licensed under the Open Government Licence v3.0."

The Alex Green, SAS Soldier Series

Future Virus

Irish Blood

Rhino

Skeleton Coast

Kano Captives

Nuclear Button

Other Novels and Short Stories

Beat The Clock

Arab Winter

Syrian Shadow

Slasher

No Gods

The Taliban & The Soldier

A Rock & A Hard Place

South Africa – Our Land!

Vigilante

Independence Day

Non-Fiction

My War

Big Sales

Printed in Great Britain
by Amazon

43493087R00118